Alfred Spates

Memorial of Alfred Spates

Contesting the Seat of Doctor Charles H. Ohr, As State Senator

Alfred Spates

Memorial of Alfred Spates
Contesting the Seat of Doctor Charles H. Ohr, As State Senator

ISBN/EAN: 9783337161576

Printed in Europe, USA, Canada, Australia, Japan

Cover: Foto ©Raphael Reischuk / pixelio.de

More available books at **www.hansebooks.com**

BY THE SENATE,

JANUARY 9th, 1867.

Referred to the Committee on Elections, and 200 copies ordered to be printed.

MEMORIAL

OF

ALFRED SPATES,

CONTESTING THE SEAT OF

DOCTOR CHARLES H. OHR,

AS STATE SENATOR.

ANNAPOLIS:

HENRY A. LUCAS, PRINTER.

1867.

MEMORIAL.

To the Honorable,

The Senate of Maryland :

The memorial of Alfred Spates, of Allegany county, Maryland, respectfully represents that he was a candidate for a seat in your body at the election of November 6th, 1866, as the representative therein of said Allegany county, and that a large number of votes at that election were cast for him for that office, and at the same time a large number of votes were cast also for Charles H. Ohr, who was returned as elected.

Your memorialist further represents that believing that said Ohr, was not duly elected to a seat in your body and designing to contest his seat, he served upon the said Ohr, a notice of his said intention, a copy of which notice is hereto annexed. He further represents that subsequent to said notice, he did, in accordance with the laws of the State of Maryland, served upon said Ohr, a notice of his intention to take testimony to substantiate his position, and thereafter, at the time fixed in said notice, he proceeded in the presence of said Ohr, to examine witnesses and take testimony, to that end, a transcrip of which testimony will by the magistrate taking the same, be transmitted to the presiding officer of your Honorable body, as required by law.

Your memorialist submits that the testimony so taken fully sustains his position and belief that the said Charles H. Ohr, was not duly elected and he therefore prays your Honorable Body to declare that said Charles H. Ohr, was not legally and duly elected, and is not therefore entitled to a seat in your Honorable Body ; but that your memorialist is the person who was duly and legally elected to such seat, at the said election of November 6th, 1866, in said Allegany county, and entitled to occupy the same.

ALFRED SPATES,
Cumberland, Allegany county, Md.

December 29th, 1866.

COPY OF NOTICE.

Allegany county, Md.

Dr. Charles H. Ohr :

SIR :—I hereby notify you that I intend to contest your seat in the Senate of Maryland, before that body when it next meets in session. I will do so on the evidence I have collected, which satisfies me that you were not fairly or legally elected Senator at the election held in Allegany county, on the 6th day of November, inst.; upon the ground that the Judges of the election in many of the election Districts, refused to reecive the ballots of a large number of registered and legal voters, who tendered their ballots to the said Judges, upon which ballots so tendered and rejected, my name was printed for Senator. And upon the ground that armed men were at the polls conspiring with the Judges and acting under the counsel of yourself, threatening force and violence, with intent to overawe and hinder the election, thereby preventing a large number of duly registered and qualified voters from casting their ballots for myself for Senator.

And upon the ground that the Judges of the election, through inadvertance or otherwise miscounted the ballots and made erroneous returns of the number of the votes cast for you and myself respectively. And upon the further ground that the Judges of the election conducted the same on, a theory which was in violation of the Constitution and laws of this State.

I have the honor to be,

Very respectfnlly,

Your obedient servant,

ALFRED SPATES.

[United States 5 ct. stamp.]

I hereby certify that I served a notice similar to the within upon Dr. Charles H. Ohr, at Cumberland, Allegany county, Maryland, on the 16th day of November, 1866.

E. J. NEAL.

[United States 5 ct. stamp.]

Sworn before me, this 23d day of November, in the year eighteen hundred and sixty-six.

J. M. STRONG, (Seal.)

Justice of the Peace of the State of Maryland,

in and for Allegany county.

[United States 5 ct. stamp.]

" EXHIBIT No. 2."

ALFRED SPATES,

vs:

DR. CHAS. H. OHR.

Summons under Code of Public General Laws, Maryland.—Contested Election.

SIR : You are hereby notified, in accordance with the provisions of section 57 of the 35th Article of the Code of Public General Laws of Maryland, that an examination of the following witnesses, viz : J. McClure Mason, Charles Best, William H. Kitzmiller, John Conneway, Jacob Gower, John Gower, Charles Nithkin, William Arnold, David A: Gower, Henry O. Hammil, Henry Hammil, Sr., Resin Turner, Francis Martin, William H. Moon, J. P. Gower, George S. Mossey, Henry Thompson, John A. Gower, Lloyd Kitzmiller, David S. Arnold, John Whirel, John Phillips, Alexander Fairall, Patrick Hammil, A. C. Hammil, George O'Brien and Richard J. West, will take place at the " Glades Hotel," kept by Mr. John Dailey, in the town of Oakland, Allegany county, Maryland, on Wednesday, the fifth day of December, 1866, at ten o'clock A. M. By these witnesses, Alfred Spates expects to prove that the said witnesses hereinbefore named were each and all citizens of Allegany county, and duly registered and legal and qualified voters in Allegany county, some of them in Election District No. 1, and the others in Election District No. 10, of said county, and entitled to vote for Senator at the election held in said county on the 6th day of November, 1866, and that said witnesses attended the election on said day, and that each and every of them, then and there, tendered and offered tickets or ballots to the Judges of said election in the election district in which they resided and in which they were duly registered as voters ; and that on said tickets or ballots so offered and tendered to the said Judges, the name of Alfred Spates was printed "For State Senator," and that said witnesses severally demanded of the Judges that said ballots or tickets should be deposited in the ballot box, and that the said Judges refused to receive the same.

And you are further notified, as aforesaid, that at the same time and place as aforesaid, there will be an examination of the following witnesses, viz :

Charles Best, Joseph Kenep, Peter Kenep, John Kenep, William Arnold and William H. Kitzmiller. By these last mentioned witnesses Alfred Spates expects to prove that you, Charles H. Ohr, was a candidate for State Senator at the election held in Allegany county on the 6th day of November, 1866, and that shortly prior to said day of election you, the

the said Charles H. Ohr, addressed a public political meeting in District No. 10, of said county, and then and there, in your said speech, counseled and advised your political friends to arm themselves on the day of election and to prevent all persons from voting at said election who were not duly registered in the year 1865. And you are further notified as aforesaid that at the same time and place first aforesaid, the following named witnesses will be examined, viz: Israel Thompson, Henry Thompson, J. McClure Mason, Charles Best, John Phillips, David S. Arnold. By these witnesses Alfred Spates expects to prove that on the day of election in District No. 10, in said county, a large number of men of radical politics were at the polls, armed with guns and pistols, and by their threats, violence and deportment intimidated and prevented a large number of the legal, registered and qualified voters of said district from offering or tendering their ballots or votes to the Judges of the election who would have voted for Alfred Spates for State Senator.

And you are further notified as aforesaid, that at the same time and place first aforesaid, the following witnesses will be examined, viz . John Beard, George N. Gower, James F. Siller, George Mossey, David E. Hauser, John Paugh, Abraham Haun, Frederick P. Sauser, Benjamin F. Shaffer, Jacob Shaffer, John N. Gower, George H. Gower, George McCormick, John C. Nithkin, Ezra Hauser, James E. Paugh, Isaiah Haun, John Ridder, Jr. John Ridder, Sr. and Elliott C. Tabb. By these witnesses Alfred Spates expects to prove that each and every of them reside in District No. 10 of Allegany county, and were duly registered as qualified voters in said election district, and that as such qualified voters they severally attended at the polls on the day of election held in Allegany county on the 6th day of November, 1866, for the purpose of voting for him, the said Alfred Spates, for State Senator, and were each and every of them prevented from voting at said election by reason of the threats and violence of a large number of armed men who were present at the polls.

And you are further notified as aforesaid, that the following named witnesses, viz : A. M. Adams, Theodore A. Ogle, Thomas E. Gonder, George W. Hoover, Henry D. Carleton, Jonn H. Young and Charles F. Bean, Deputy Clerk of the Circuit Court for Allegany county, will be examined at the Court house, in the city of Cumberland, on Monday, the 10th day of December, 1866, at 11 o'clock. By these last named witnesses Alfred Spates expects to prove that the said witnesses did, on the 17th day of November, 1866, in the Clerk's office in Allegany county, in the presence of the Clerk of the Circuit Court, carefully count all the tickets and ballots voted in each and every of the election districts in Allegany county at the election held on the 6th day of November, 1866 ; and that upon said careful count they found that twenty-three hundred and forty-two votes or ballots had been cast or voted for the said Alfred Spates for State Senator and twenty-three hundred and seven votes had been cast or voted for you, the said Charles H. Ohr, for State Senator ; and that the tickets or ballots so counted were the same tickets and ballots which had been returned by the Judges of said election and lodged with the Clerk of the Circuit Court for Allegany county under the provisions of section 38 of Article 35 of the Code of Public General Laws of Maryland ; and that the Judges of the election of Election District No. 5 of Allegany county did not return any certificate of the number of votes cast for State Senator in said district under the provisions of section 28 of Article 35 of the Public General Laws of Maryland.

If all the witnesses cannot be examined in the days named then to be continued from day to day until the same is through.

You are required to attend at the above mentioned times and places either in person or by attorney to cross-examine witnesses.

Given under my hand and seal, this 23d day of November, 1866.

J. M. STRONG,   [SEAL.]

Justice of the Peace of the State of Maryland,

in and for Allegany county.

U. S. 50 ct. stamp.

I hereby certify that I served a notice similar to the within upon Dr. Charles H. Ohr, at Cumberland, Allegany county, Maryland, on the 23d day of November, 1866.

E. J. SEAL.

[U. S. 5 ct. stamp.]

Sworn to before me, this 23d day of November, in the year of our Lord, eighteen hundred and sixty-six.

J. M. STRONG   [SEAL.]

Justice of the Peace of the State of Maryland,

in and for Allegany county.

[United States 5 ct. stamp.]

COUNTER MEMORIAL OF C. H. OHR.

To the Honorable,

    The Senate of Maryland :

The answer and counter memorial of C. H. Ohr. to the memorial of Alfred Spates, contesting the election of this respondent, as Senator for Allegany county.

This respondent admits that at the election held for State

Senator for said county, on the 6th of November, 1866, the said Spates was a candidate for State Senator, and received a large number of votes for that office; and that a larger number of votes were cast at the said election for this respondent for said office, and that he was declared by the judges of said election, to be duly elected as such Senator.

This respondent further admits that the said Spates, on the 16th of November, 1866, did serve on this respondent, notice of his intention to contest the election of this respondent, and also on the 23d of said month, delivered a notice of the witnesses and time, and place, where he would take testimony to substantiate his claims to the seat of this respondent.

In the said notice, the said contestant alleges four grounds of contest to be proven by said witness. Your respondent submits that the testimony produced by the said contestant, fails to substantiate any one of these alleged grounds as applicable to this contest, and that by the rebutting testimony of this respondent, on due notice according to the requirements of the Code of Public General Laws, the contestant's claim is wholly disproven.

This respondent further respectfully submits, that the said contestant is disqualified by the Constitution and Laws of this State, for the said office, and being thus ineligible, he could not, even if he had received a majority of the votes cast at said election, be entitled to a seat in the Senate, and that the votes cast for him must be thrown away, and that many of said votes were illegally cast; the voters themselves not possessing the legal qualifications entitling them to exercise the elective franchise.

All of which is respectfuly submitted,
C. H. OHR.

"EXIBIT No. 3."

STATE OF MARYLAND,
ALLEGANY COUNTY, to wit:

I hereby certify that it appears on records in this office, that Alfred Spates, was duly registered as a voter in District No. 6, in Allegany county, Maryland, in the year 1865; and that his name, as such registered voter, appears upon the registry book of said District No. 6, in said county, and also on the return of the registers, filed in the clerk's office for record; as directed by the Act of Assembly, in such cases made and provided:

In testimony whereof, I hereto subscribe my name
[SEAL.] and affix the Seal of the Circuit Court for
Allegany County, this 27th day of November, 1866,

H. RESLEY,
Clerk of the Circuit Court,
for Allegany County.

[U. S. 5 ct. Stamp.]

"EXHIBIT No. 5."

A certified copy of the list of voters who voted at the election in District No. 10, Allegany county, on the 6th day of Nov. 1866, as taken from the books of the Polls returned to the Clerk's office by the Judges of election of that District, Nov. 10th, 1866.

1 Wovrell, N. B.
2 Biggs, M. S.
3 Lee, James H.
4 Lee, George S.
5 Chisholm, James,
6 Chisholm, Archibald, Jr.
7 Chisholm, Archibald, Sr.
8 Wilson, George W.
9 Sollars, John W.
10 Waltz, William,
11 Harvey, Benjamin F.
12 Harvey, M. S.
13 Harvey, Crampton,
14 Biggs, William H.
15 Chisholm, Alexander,
16 Harvey, Thomas K.
17 Crim, Joseph M.
18 Yutzy, Jacob,
19 Sollars, William,
20 Sanders, Henry G.
21 Miller, Peter,
22 Thompson, Isaac J.
23 Shrought, B. A.
24 Wilson, William J.
25 White, John M.
26 Wildeson, Wm. C.
27 Biggs, Upton F.
28 Harvey, Hoah,

42 Moon, Hugh,
43 Moon, Joseph,
44 Blample, John,
45 Rolf, William,
46 Moon, John,
47 Moon, Martin,
48 Moon, William,
49 Moon, Isaac,
50 Moon, Garret V.
51 Thompson, Israel,
52 Harvey, N. B.
53 Lee, Henry,
54 Kneff, Henry,
55 Lee, Federick,
56 White, James J.
57 Styer, John G.
58 Bucy, William A.
59 Kitsmiller, Alexander,
60 Gauer, Adam,
61 Gauer, John H.
62 Stilley, Arust,
63 Shaffer, John M. B.
64 Lee, Robert,
65 Kneff, John,
66 Moon, Thomas,
67 Yutzy, Christian,
68 Nydigger, Lewis,
69 Lish, Charles,

2

29 White, James W.
30 Riley, Thomas,
31 White, James H.
32 Harvey, John O.
33 Moon, Benjamin,
34 Harvey, James W.
35 Moon, Jeremiah,
36 Irous, Joseph,
37 Harvey, John W.
38 Shaffer, Thomas J.
39 Moon, John T.
40 Chisholm, Daniel,
41 Harvey, Elisha,

70 Riley, John G. C.
71 Walter, George J.
72 Worrall, Thomas,
73 Harvey, William,
74 Wilt, David,
75 Harvey, Elisha, Sr.
76 Yutzy, Soloman,
77 Lee, William,
78 White, William B.
79 Lee, John W.
80 Paugh, Phillip H.
81 Shaffer, John,
82 Anderson, Jacob V.

State of Maryland, Allegany County, to wit :

I, Horace Resley, Clerk of the Circuit Court for Allegany county, do hereby certify the above and foregoing to be truly taken from the books of the Polls, returned to the Clerk's office by the Judges of election of District No. 10, Nov. 10, 1866.

In testimony whereof I hereunto set my hand and affix the seal of said Court, this 24th day of November, 1866.

[SEAL.]   HORACE RESLEY,
                    Clerk of the Circuit Court for,
                        Allegany county.
[U. S. 5 ct. Stamp.]

"EXHIBIT No. 6."

To the Clerk of the

Circuit Court, for Allegany County:

WHEREAS, an election for a Comptroller of the State of Maryland, one Member of the House of Representatives in the Congress of the United States for the fourth Congressional District of Maryland: One Senator for Allegany county to the State Senate, and five Members of the House of Delegates; was held on the first Tuesday succeeding the first Monday of November, being the sixth day of said month, in the year eighteen hundred and sixty-six, in the several Election Districts, in the said Allegany county, distinguished by members from No. (1) one to No. (16) sixteen inclusive, conformably to the Constitution and Laws of this State; and whereas, we the subscribers attending Judges at the close of the election in said Districts, having this day assembled at the usual place of the sitting of the Circuit Court for said county, with the books of the polls, on which are endorsed the several certificates agreeably to law, and having cast up the whole number of votes given in said Districts, according to the certificates made out on the day of election by the Judges, it appears that Col. Robert Bruce, had twenty-four hundred and ten (2410) votes for Comptroller, Col. William J. Leonard, had twenty-two hundred and ninety-two (2292) votes for Comptroller; Francis Thomas had twenty-three hundred and seventy-six, (2376) votes for Representative in Congress; Col. William P. Maulsby, had twenty-three hundred and eight (2308) votes for Representative in Congress; Charles H. Ohr had twenty-three hundred and thirty-seven (2337) votes for Senator; Alfred Spates had twenty-three hundred and twenty-five (2325) votes for Senator; William R. McCulley had twenty-three hundred and ninety-nine (2399) votes for the House of Delegates; Charles Gilpin had twenty-three hundred and eighty (2380) votes for the House of Delegates; Samuel M. Haller had twenty-three hundred and fifty-nine (2359) votes for the House of Delegates; Daniel C. Bruce, had twenty-three hundred and ninety-six votes for the House of Delegates; William A. Falkenstine, had twenty-three hundred and five(2305) votes for the House of Delegates; George W. McCulloh, had twenty-three hundred and fifty-six (2356) votes for the House of Delegates; Patrick Hamill, had twenty-three hundred and seven (2307) votes for the House of Delegates; William Devecmon, had twenty-three hundred and thirty-six (2336) votes for the House of Delegates; John McElfish had twenty-two hundred and ninety-seven votes, for the House of Delegates; William A. Brydon, had twenty-three hundred and thirty-four (2334) votes for the House of Delegates. Whereupon we do determine, declare and return that Robert Bruce had the highest number of legal votes for Comptroller. Francis Thomas had the highest number of legal votes for Congress; Charles H. Ohr had the highest number of legal votes, and is duly elected Senator, and that William R. McCulley, Daniel C. Bruce, Charles Gilpin, George W. McCulloh and Samuel M. Haller had the highest number of legal votes for the House of Delegates, and are duly elected Delegates.

We further certify, that twenty hundred and thirteen (2013) votes were cast in favor of the Constitutional amendment, and thirteen hundred and fifty-one (1351) votes were cast against the Constitutional amendment, and that twelve hundred and fifty-six (1256) votes were cast in favor of the county school tax, and one hundred and seventeen (117) votes were cast against the county school tax.

Given under our hands this 10th day of November, 1866.

Samuel W. Friend,	District No. 1
David Kent,	District No. 2
G. W. Layman,	District No. 3
E. C. Lyons,	District No. 4
Wm Conrad.	District No. 5
John Boward,	District No. 6
Loyd Stallings,	District No. 7
James T. Hartley,	District No. 8
John Fletcher,	District No. 9
James Chisholm,	District No. 10
Joseph De Witt,	Distr
Lewis Pritchard,	District No. 12
Joseph M. Koerner,	District No. 13
John Brady,	District No. 14
Ralph Thayer,	District No. 15
John Picken,	District No. 16

STATE OF MARYLAND,

ALLEGANY COUNTY, *to wit:*

I hereby certify, that the above and aforegoing is a true copy of the return of the Judges of election for the several Election Districts in Allegany county, of the votes polled at the election held on the sixth day of November, in the year eighteen hundred and sixty-six.

[SEAL.]   In testimony whereof, I hereunto subscribe my name and affix the seal of the Circuit Court for Allegany county, Maryland, this twenty-ninth day of November, in the year of our Lord, eighteen hundred and sixty-six.

HORACE RESLEY,

Clerk.

[U. S. 5 ct. stamp.]

"EXHIBIT No. 7."

STATE OF MARYLAND,

ALLEGANY COUNTY, to wit:

I hereby certify, that the Registers of voters for District number ten, in Allegany county, Maryland, to wit: William R. Sollers, George S. Lee and Upton F. Biggs, appointed by the Governor of Maryland, for the year 1865, in accordance with the Constitution and laws of the State of Maryland, they did not, they nor either of them, file their commissions as

Registers, with the Clerk of the Circuit Court, for the County aforesaid, within the time required by law, nor did they, or either of them, take the oath of office before said Clerk, or any of his sworn deputies as required by law

I further certify, that the aforesaid Registers, to wit: William R. Sollers, George S. Lee and Upton F. Biggs, did not. nor did either of them, at any time within the period required by law, nor at any time thereafter, file or lodge with the Clerk aforesaid, a copy of the register of qualified voters to be recorded by said Clerk according to law, as required by section 12, of Chapter 174, passed at January Session 1865.

In testimony whereof, I hereunto subscribe my
[SEAL] name, and affix the seal of the Circuit Court for Allegany county, this 10th day of December, 1866.

H. RESLEY,
Clerk of the Circuit Court for
Allegany County.

[U. S. 5 ct. stamp.]

"EXHIBIT No. 8."

A certified copy of the list of voters who voted at the election in District No. 1, in Allegany county, on the 6th of November, 1866, as taken from the books of the Polls, returned to the Clerk's Office by the Judges of Election of that District, November 10, 1866.

1 John Friend,	60 John Gankey,
2 E. G. Blackburn,	61 S. W. Friend,
3 Henry E. Friend,	62 Ebernezer Kitzmiller,
4 John Edgar,	63 Thornton Gilpin, Sr.,
5 Abraham McCroby,	64 Benjamin Davis,
6 William A. Falkenstine,	65 Thomas D. Paugh,
7 Winfield S. Friend,	66 John A. Droege,
8 William Sharpless,	67 William H. H. Friend,
9 Harman Beckman,	68 John Paugh, Sr.,
10 Gilbert W. Turner,	69 William Upole,
11 Solomon Turner,	70 Richard Tasker, Sr.,
12 John Miller,	71 Joseph Paugh, Jr.,
13 Abraham Hershberger,	72 Levi Comp,
14 Lawrence Clyens,	73 Ebernezer B. Davis,
15 Nelson Savage,	74 Henry Tasker,
16 John McCroby,	75 Samuel Jones,
17 E. P. Town,	76 John Fitzwater,
18 Solomon B. Harvey,	77 Jeremiah Tasker,
19 Joseph Knox,	78 Solomon Tasker,
20 Benjamin Blackburn,	79 Jacob Spiker,

21 Benjamin Friend,	80 John W. Harvey,
22 James Dolan,	81 Joseph Welch,
23 Josiah F. Murphy,	82 Richard H. Johnson,
24 Benjamin G. Spiker,	83 Joshua W. Dimmitt,
25 John Maley,	84 Henry Bray,
26 Michael Welch,	85 William Swartzwelder,
27 Patrick Haniley.	86 Francis M. McGroby,
28 John Woods,	87 William H. Wilson,
29 Lewis Kleigel,	88 John Wilt,
30 William H. Rhodes.	89 Peter Wilt,
31 Otho Willis,	90 Samson Harvey,
32 Abraham J. Wilson,	91 Josiah G. Friend,
33 Jonathan H. Wilson,	92 Phillip Dufford,
34 Thomas Kelly,	93 Thomas Burke,
35 John Beckman,	94 Theophilus Wilt,
36 John Beckman, Sr.,	95 John Roan,
37 James Davis,	96 A. F. Harvey,
38 George Britts,	97 Thaddeus Vanderhoof,
39 Benjamin G. Sharretts,	98 Elijah Howel,
40 Elisha D. McCroby,	99 William Schooley,
41 William T. Harvey,	100 Joseph F. Friend,
42 Michael McCroby,	101 John W. Ellis,
43 Daniel Wilson,	102 Emanuel Dennis,
44 Milford B. Hagans,	103 Hampton McCrobie,
45 James Wilson,	104 Michael Garrett,
46 Jefferson Stull,	105 Laurence Staunton,
47 Henry C. McCroby,	106 John Wagner,
48 William Coffman,	107 Samuel B. Harvey,
49 Andrew F. McCroby,	108 Samuel Warnick,
50 Nathaniel B. Harvey,	109 James Z. Browning,
51 Lewis F. Paugh,	110 Joseph P. Mongar,
52 Jhon S. Hileman,	111 John A. Jenkins,
53 David J. Beavers,	112 Samuel Rodyhufer,
54 Andrew J. Rodes,	113 Michael F. Paugh,
55 Meshack Harvey,	114 Joseph H. Paugh,
56 William H. Baugh,	115 James M. Wagner,
57 Williiam H. Hoye,	116 John F. Harvey,
58 Mannassa G. Harvey,	117 Joshua J. Mason,
59 William W. Bray,	118 Silas Fitzwater,

STATE OF MARYLAND,

ALLEGANY COUNTY, to wit:

I, Horace Resley, Clerk of Circuit Court for Allegany county, do hereby certify, that the above and aforegoing, to be truly taken from the books of the Polls for District No. 1, in Allegany county, Maryland.

In testimony whereof, I hereunto set my hand [SEAL] and affix the seal of said Court, this 26th day of November, 1866.   HORACE RESLEY,
Clerk of the Circuit Court for

[U. S. 5 ct. stamp.]   Allegany County.

"EXHIBIT No. 9."

A certified list of the Registered Voters in District No. 10., in Allegany county, Maryland, as returned by the Registers for the years 1865 and 1866.

1 Abernathy, James W.	72 Moon, Isaac
2 Abernathy, David	73 Moon, John F.
3 Arnold, William	74 Moon, Joseph
4 Arnold, David S.	75 Moon, Thomas
5 Anderson, Jacob V.	76 Moon, Jacob K.
6 Biggs, Middleton S.	77 Moon, John
7 Biggs, Upton F.	78 Moon, Josiah
8 Bucy, William A.	79 Moon, Benjamin Jr.
9 Biggs, William H.	80 Moon, Garret V.
10 Best, Charles	81 Moon, Hugh
11 Blampal, John	82 Miller, Peter
12 Beard, John	83 Moon, Martin
13 Chisholm, James Sr.,	84 McCormick, George
14 Chisholm, Archibald Sr.,	85 Martin, Francis
15 Chisholm, Archibald Jr.	86 Mossey, George L.
16 Chisholm, Alexandria	87 Moon, Jeremiah
17 Chisholm, Daniel	88 Mossey, George
18 Crim, Joseph M.	89 Moon, William
19 Conneway, John	90 Mason, J. McClure
20 Fike, David	91 Mydeger, Lewis
21 Fogalpole, Rudolph	92 Milliken, Charles O.
22 Gartner, Peter	93 Milliken, John C.
23 Gower, Jacob of A	94 Paugh, Phillip H.
24 Gower, Adam	95 Paugh, John
25 Gower, John W.	96 Phillips, John
26 Gower, David A.	97 Paugh, James E.
27 Gower, Jacob I.	98 Riley, John G. C.
28 Gower, John	99 Riley, Thomas A.
29 Gower, John N.	100 Roth, John
30 Gower, George N.	101 Roth, John G.
31 Gower, John A.	102 Ridder, John Sr.
32 Gower, George H.	103 Rolf, William
33 Harvey, Nathaniel B.	104 Ridder, John Jr.
34 Harvey, James W.	105 Roth, George
35 Harvey, Elisha Jr.,	106 Sollars, William P.
36 Harvey, John O.	107 Sollars, John W.
37 Harvey, Elisha Jr.	108 Sanders, Henry G.
38 Harvey, Reason	109 Sanders, John F.
39 Harvey, Thomas K	110 Shaffer, John
40 Harvey, Michael S.	111 Steyer, John G.
41 Harvey, Noah	112 Shrought, Beckwarth A.
42 Hawn, Abraham	113 Shaffer, Thomas G.
43 Hawn, Isaiah	114 Stily, Adam
44 Harvey, Benjamin F.	115 Saucer, Frederick P.

45 Harvey, John W.	116 Shaffer, Jacob
46 Harvey, William	117 Shaffer, Benjamin F.
47 Hauser, David E.	118 Shaffer, John M. B.
48 Hauser, Ezra	119 Shaffer, Henry A.
49 Harvey, Crampton	120 Thompson, Isaac J.
o 1Iuse, Joseph	121 Thompson, Israel
51 Kenep, Joseph	122 Tabb, Elliot C.
52 Kenep, Henry	123 Thompson, Henry
53 Kitzmiller, Alexander	124 White, James J.
54 Kenep, Peter	125 White, James W.
55 Kenep, John	126 White, John M.
56 Kiltsmiller, Lloyd	127 White, William B.
57 Kiltsmiller, William H.	128 White, James H.
58 Lee, Frederick	129 Worrall, Thomas
59 Lee, Dudley	130 Wilson, William J.
60 Lee, George S.	131 Worral, Norman B.
61 Lee, John W.	132 Wilson, George W.
62 Lee, James H.	133 Walter, George J.
63 Lee, Henry	134 Waltz, William
64 Lowry, Henry	135 Wilt, David
65 Lowery, Enoch	136 Wimer, John
66 Lechit, Jesse	137 Walter, Henry
67 Lish, Charles	138 Wildersen, William
68 Liller, James F.	139 Whirell, John I.
69 Lee Robert	140 Yutzy, Jacob
70 Lee, William	141 Yutzy, Christian
71 Moon, William H.	142 Yutzy, Solomon

STATE OF MARYLAND,

ALLEGANY COUNTY, *to wit :*

I Horace Resley, Clerk of the Circuit Court for Allegany county, do hereby certify the above and aforegoing to be truly taken from the book of Registration for District No. 10, Allegany county, Md.

[SEAL.] In testimony whereof, I hereunto set my hand and affix the Seal of said Court this 24th day of November, 1866,

HORACE RESLEY,
Clerk of the Circuit Court for
Allegany County.

[U. S. 5 ct. stamp.]

"EXHIBIT No. 10."

A certified list of the Registered Voters in District No. 1, in Allegany county, Maryland, as returned by the Registers, for the years 1865 and 1866:

B.
Bray John,
Beckman, John Jr.
Bever, David J.
Browning, James Z.
Bray, William W.
Rurke, Thomas
Blackburn, B. F.
Beckman, John, Sr.
Blackburn, E. G.
Beckman. Harman,

C
Coffman, William C:
Clyens, Lawrence
Comp, Levi

D
Droege John A.
Dimmitt, Joshua W.
Dolan, James T.
Doffert, Philip
Davis, James
Davis, Ebenezer
Davis, Benjamin
Dennis, Emmanuel

E
Edgar John
Ellis, John W.

F
Friend, Joseph F.
Friend, Benjamin F.
Friend, William H. H.
Friend, Josiah G.
Friend, John
Falkenstein, William A.
Freelin, Abraham
Friend, Samuel W.
Fitzwater, Silas
Fitzwater, John L.
Fairall. Alexander
Friend, Henry E.
Friend, Wingfield S.

G
Gilpen, Thornton
Garrett, Michael

H
Harvey, Lewis F.
Harvey, John T.
Harvey, William L.
Harvey, John W.
Heshburger, Abraham
Harvy, Samuel P.
Harvey. A. F.
Hoye, William H.
Harvy, Joseph S.
Harvy, Nathaniel B.
Harvy, Sampson
Harvey, Shadrick
Harvy, Meshach
Harvy, Mannasseh G.
Howel, Jefferson
Howel, William
Howel, Elijah
Hagans, Milford B.
Hammill, Patrick
Haumill, Henry O.
Hammill, Archibald C.
Hanily, Patrick
Harvy, Solomon B.
Hammill, Henry
Hileman, John S.

J
Jones, Samuel
Jones, George
Johnson, Richard H.
Jankey, John
Jenkins, John A.

K
Kope, John H.
Kitzmiller, Ebenezer
Knox, Joseph
Kirkpatrick, John S.
Kilgallen, James
Kelly, Thomas
Klegel, Lewis Sr.
Kitzmiller, John H.

L
Laughridge, John M.
Lee, Abraham

3

M

Murphy, Josiah F.
Mason, Joshua J.
Maley, John
Miller, John
Mangar, Joseph P.
McKenzie, Henry C.
McCrobie, John
McCrobie, Francis. M.
McCrobie, Elisha D.
McCrobie, Abraham A.
McCrobie, Thomas B.
McCrobie, Michael
McCrobie Hampton
McCrobie, A. F.

O

O'Brine, George

P

Paugh, William H.
Paugh, Joseph H.
Paugh, Joseph, Sr.
Paugh, Michael T.
Paugh, William H. Jr.
Paugh, Tomas D.
Paugh, Lewis F.
Pritts, George
Paugh, John Sr.

R

Rhodes, Andrew S.
Rodehauver, Samuel
Roads, William H.
Rowan, John

S

Schooley, William
Swartzwelder, William
Spiker, Benjamin G.
Spikes, Jacob

Savage, Nelson
Sharpless, William
Staunton, Lawrence
Sharaetts, B. S.
Stull, Jefferson C.

T

Tasker, Richard
Tasker, Henry R.
Tasker, Solomon
Tasker, Joseph
Tasker, Jeremiah
Town, E. P.
Turner, Gilbert W.
Turner, Solomon
Turner, Reason

U

Upole, William

V

Vanderhoof, Thaddeus

W

Wilt, John
Wilt, Peter
Waruick, Samuel
Willis, Otho
Wilson, James
Wilson, Daniel
Wilson, Abraham J.
Wilson, William H.
Wilt, John H.
Wilt, Theopolis
Wilson, Jonathan H.
Wagner, John
Wagner, James M.
Woads, John
Welsh, Michael
West, Richard J.
Welch, Joseph

STATE OF MARYLAND,
     ALLEGANY COUNTY, *to wit :*
I Horace Resley, Clerk of the Circuit Court for Allegany
county, do hereby certify the above and aforegoing to be truly
taken from the book of Regsitration for Election District No. 1.
                    In testimony whereof, I hereunto set my hand
     [SEAL.]   and affix the seal of said Court this 26th day
                 of November, 1866.
                         HORACE RESLEY,
                    Clerk of the Circuit Court for
                              Allegany county.

[U. S. 5 ct. stamp.]

"EXHIBIT No. 11."

We, the undersigned duly appointed in due form of law Judges of the Election in District No. 5, of Allegany county, Maryland, do hereby certify and return that we did attend on the first Tuesday in November, in the year of our Lord one thousand eight hundred and sixty-six, at the place by law appointed for holding the election within said district, and did then and there appoint R. W. Mason and John C. Weis, Clerks of the Election, who severally qualified as directed by law. We further certify that we did then and there qualify as Judges of the Election as by law directed, and did then and there, at the hour of nine o'clock in the morning, open the polls for an election for a Comptroller, for one Representative in Congress, for one State Senator, for five delegates for House of Delegates, and for, and against the Amendment to the Constitution; that we continued the polls open until six o'clock in the evening of the said day, when they were closed, the ballot box opened and the ballots publicly counted, when it appeared that Col. Robert Bruce had four hundred and four votes, and Colonel William J. Leonard two hundred and ninety-five votes for Comptroller, and Francis Thomas had four hundred and one votes and Col. William P. Maulsby two hundred and ninety-five votes for Congress, and Col. Charles Gilpin had four hundred and two votes, Wm. R. McCulley four hundred and four votes, Samuel M. Haller had three hundred and ninety-two votes, Daniel C. Bruce had four hundred and fourteen votes, and Captain Wm. A. Falkenstein had three hundred and seventy-five votes; Patrick Hamill had two hundred and ninety-three votes, G. W. McCulloh had three hundred and thirty-six votes, and Wm. Devecmon had two hundred and ninety-seven votes, William A. Bryden had two hundred and ninety-three votes, and John McElfish had two hundred and eighty-nine votes for the House of Delegates, and for the Amendment three hundred and two votes, and against the Amendment ninety-seven votes.

Given under our hands at the place of said election this sixth day of November, in the year of our Lord one thousand eight hundred and sixty-six.

Attested by   WM. CONRAD, R. J.,
R. W. MASON,   ⎰ Judges.   WM. STAPES,
JNO. C. WEIS.   ⎱   BENJ. THOMAS.

[NOTE.—By reference to the above return made and signed by the Judges of Election in District No. 5, it will be seen that no mention is made of the vote received by Alfred Spates or Charles H. Ohr for Senator, as provided under the 28th section of 35th Article of the Public General Laws of Maryland.]

STATE OF MARYLAND,

ALLEGANY COUNTY, TO WIT:

I hereby certify that the above and aforegoing is truly taken from the election returns made by the Judges of Election District No. 5, of the election held November 6, 1866, in Allegany county, Maryland, and that the same is a true copy of such certificate and return annexed to the poll books of election of said Election District No. 5. returned and filed as aforesaid in the office of the Clerk of the Circuit Court for Allegany county, Maryland, on the 10th of November, 1866.

In testimony whereof I hereunto subscribe my name and affix the seal of the Circuit Court for Allegany county, Maryland, this first day of December, in the year eighteen hundred and sixty-six.

[SEAL.]   HORACE RESLEY,

Clerk of Circuit Court for Allegany county, Md.
[U. S. 5 ct. Stamp.]

For Comptroller.

Col. Wm. J. Leonard,	299	Votes.
Col. Robert Bruce,	404	"

For Congress.

Francis Thomas,	401	"
Col. Wm. P. Maulsby,	295	"

For State Senator.

Charles H. Ohr,	399	"
Col. Alfred Spates,	296	"

For House of Delegates.

Chas. Gilpin,	402	"
W. A. Faulkenstein,	375	"
Wm. R. McCulley,	404	"
Samuel M. Haller,	392	"
Daniel C. Bruce.	414	"
P. Hamill,	293	"
George W. McCulloh,	336	"
Wm. Devecmon,	297	"
Wm. A. Bryden,	293	"
John McElfish,	289	"
For Amendment,	302	"
Against Amendment,	97	"

"TALLY LIST,"

Of recounted tickets at the Clerk's office, Allegany county, Maryland, Nov. 17, 1866.

DISTRICTS.	C. H. OHR. Count of Judges.	Re-count.	DISTRICTS.	COL. A. SPATES. Count of Judges.	Re-count.
No. 1,		69	No. 1,		49
" 2		116	" 2		62
" 3		155	" 3		127
" 4		223	" 4		226
" 5	(399)	390	" 5	(296)	307
" 6	(225)	219	" 6	(352)	355
" 7	(53)	52	" 7		83
" 8	(45)	44	" 8		58
" 9		103	" 9		114
" 10		69	" 10		13
" 11		68	" 11		35
" 12	(102)	101	" 12		196
" 13	(383)	372	" 13	(449)	452
" 14		78	" 14		12
" 15		96	" 15		77
" 16	(153)	152	" 16		136

Cumberland, Nov. 17, 1866.   THE. A. OGLE.

Total number of votes cast for Col. Alfred Spates,   2342.
Total number of votes cast for Charles H. Ohr,   2307.

Majority for Col. Alfred Spates,   35

Note.—The figures in () are the count made by the Judges of election ; those *not in* () are the count made this day, Nov. 17th 1866, by the persons named below :

Henry D. Carleton,
John H. Young,
A. M. Adams,
· Thos. E. Gonder,
Theo. A. Ogle,
Geo. W. Hoover.

CUMBERLAND, ALLEGANY CO., MD.,

December 29th, 1866.

To the Presiding Officer of the
Senate of the State of Maryland:

SIR :—In accordance with the provisions of the 61st section of the 35th Article of the Maryland Code of Public General Laws, I herewith transmit the certificates of notice and proof of the service of the same, and the depositions taken in the contested election case therein named.

Respectfully,

J. M. STRONG, [SEAL.]

Justice of the Peace of the
State of Maryland, in and
for Allegany county.

[U. S. 5 cts. Stamp.]

ALFRED SPATES, }

vs. } Before the Senate of Mary-
} land.

DR. CHARLES H. OHR. }

Depositions taken before me, Joseph M. Strong, a Justice of the Peace of the State of Maryland, in and for Allegany county:

Be it remembered, and I hereby certify, that on the twenty-third day of November, 1866, was filed with me a paper containing a notice, certificate and affidavit ; which paper is herewith filed, marked "Exhibit No. 1."

(See "Exhibit No. 1.")

And on the day of the filing with me by Alfred Spates, of the paper aforesaid, the said Alfred Spates applied to me, Joseph M. Strong, Justice as aforesaid, to take testimony to be used in the above entitled case.

And thereupon, I issued the following notice, to wit, with certificate and affidavit endorsed thereon, and herewith filed as part of this record, and marked "Exhibit No. 2," and which, with all other exhibits herewith also filed, is to be taken and considered as part of this record.

(See "Exhibit No. 2.")

J. M. STRONG, [SEAL.]
Justice of the Peace of the
State of Maryland, in and
for Allegany county.

[U. S. 5 cts. Stamp.]

Names of Persons Registered.	Sworn.	His Age	Place of Birth.	Time he has resided in Allegany county.	Date of Naturalization Papers and Court in which naturalized. Date.	Court.	Cause or Reason of Disqualification.	Names of Qualified Voters.
District No. 1. 1866. Henry O. Hamill. Henry Hamill.							Generally believed disloyal. Disloyal by the testimony of witnesses Fitzwater Silas, Abraham Harshburger and others.	
George O'Brien.							Disloyal by giving aid and comfort—witness, Fitzwater, F. Duffort and others.	
District No. 1. 1866, August 7th. Henry O. Hamill. Henry Hamill.	Sworn. "	62 67	Maryland. Ireland.	9 years. 43 years.	17th Oct., 1861.	Cumberland, Md.	Testimony for H. Hamill, S. Fitzwater and others. He said he gave some men something to eat at the time of Jones' raid, and said he would give any man something to eat, and I don't think he meant it for disloyalty to the U. S. Government, and I believe he is loyal to his Country and others.	Henry O. Hamill.
1866, Sept. 12th, George O'Brien.	"	30	Maryland.	30 years.			Testimony of S. Fitzwater—said he gave West and Jasker something to eat, but did not think he was doing anything wrong; and he did not tell me he harbored them, and I think he is loyal.	Henry Hamill. George O. Brien.
District No. 2. 1865. Jeremiah Guard. Peter Spealman. Otho Spealman. John Slicer, Sr. Richard White. 1866.	Absent. " " " "		Moved to Gruntsville, Md.				Disloyal—Witnesses, Jno. Augustson, Geo. W. Rileman. Disloyal—Witnesses, Samuel Hilleman, L. D Hoff and others. Disloyal—Witnesses, Sam'l Williams, L. D. Hoff and others. Disloyal—Witnesses, Geo. A. Fearer, R. B. White and others. Disloyal—Witnesses, Jno. E. Frazer, Geo. A. Fearer and 20 others.	
District No. 2. Jeremiah Guard. Peter Spealman. Otho Spealman. Richard White. 1865.	affirmed. " " Sworn.	52. 75. 33. 72.	Allegany county, Md Frederick county, Md. Allegany county, Md. " " "	52 years. 75 years. 33 years. 72 years.				Jeremiah Guard. Peter Spealman. Otho Spealman. Richard White.
District No. 5. Henry Klein. 1866.	"		Prussia.		1856.	Allegany county, Md.	Disloyal—Refused to take the oath.	
District No. 5. Henry Klein. 1865.	"	45.	Prussia.	16 years.	1866.	Allegany county, Md.		Henry Klein.
District No. 10. David S. Arnold. Charles Best. William H. Kitzmiller. James Liller. William Moon. J. McLure Mason. John Phillips. John Ridder, Sr. Benj. F. Shaffer. Henry Thompson. 1866.							Rejoiced over Southern victory—Witnesses, Wm. Waltz and J. W. Lee. Rejoiced over Rebel victory—Witnesses, Wm. Waltz, John J. Moon. Disloyal—Witnesses, John Weimer, Wm. Waltz. Disloyal—Joseph Moon. Rejoiced over Rebel victory—Alexander Chisholm. Disloyal, general reputation—John W. Lee, James W. Harvey. Disloyal—Witnesses, Upton F. Riggs, Wm. Waltz, T. Moon. Disloyal—Witnesses, Geo. S. Lee, W. R. Sollers. Refused to take the oath.	
District No. 10. David S. Arnold. Charles Best. Wm. H. Kitzmiller. James F. Liller. William Moon. J. McLure Mason. John Phillips. John Ridder, Sr. Benj. F. Shaffer. Henry Thompson. 1865. **District No. 14.** Wm. Browning, Sr.	Sworn. " " " " " " " " Affirmed. Sworn.	36 54 34 28 66 60 62 69 25 46 60	Maryland England. Virginia. Virginia. Maryland. Virginia. Maryland. Germany. Maryland. Maryland. Allegany Co., Md.	36 years. 17 years. 12 years. 6 years. 65 years. 25 years. 52 years. 36 years. 25 years. 60 years.	May 9, 1849. Oct., 1837.	Hudson county, N. Y. Cumberland, Md.	Disloyalty under the 4th sec. of Art. 1st of the Constitution—Witnesses, Archibald Castel, William McCabe, P. H. McCabe and others.	David S. Arnold. Charles Best. Wm. H. Kitzmiller. James F. Liller. William Moon. J. McLure Mason. John Phillips. John Ridder, Sr. Benj. F. Shaffer. Henry Thompson.
Thomas Browning. Walter Wilburn.							Disloyalty under the 4th sec. of Art. 1st of the Constitution—Witness, Jas. Browning. Disloyalty under the 4th sec. of Art. 1st of the Constitution—Witnesses, Singleton J. Wilburn and Thomas Wilburn.	
1865. **District No. 14.** Wm. Browning, Sr. Thomas Browning. Walter Wilburn. 1866. **District No. 3.** John Slicer, Sr.	Sworn. " " Sworn.	61 49 90 63	Allegany Co., Md. " " " P. George's Co., Md. Virginia.	61 years. 49 years. 35 years. 62 years.				William Browning, Sr. Thomas Browning. Walter Wilburn. John Slicer, Sr.

MARYLAND, Allegany County, } ss.

I hereby certify that the aforegoing is a true copy of the entries and erasures, as taken from the Books of Registration of the different Election Districts in the State and County aforesaid, to wit: Districts Nos. 1, 2, 5, 10 and 14, as returned to the Clerk's Office in the County aforesaid by the Officers of Registration of said Districts, for the years 1865 and 1866.

Witness my hand and official seal, this 1st day of January, 1867.

[SEAL.]

H. RESLEY,
Clerk Circuit Court for Allegany County.

TESTIMONY.

OAKLAND, ALLEGANY CO., MD.,
December 5th, 1866.

In pursuance of the aforegoing notice, I attended at the time and place first therein designated, and having appointed James J. McHenry, as Clerk, and administered to him an oath to fairly write down and transcribe the depositions to be taken by me, did proceed then and there to take the following testimony, to wit :

Deposition No. 1.

PATRICK HAMMIL having been duly sworn, deposed and said as follows, to wit :

By Mr. Spates :

Question. What is your name, age, occupation and residence; and how long have you resided there?

Answer. My name is Patrick Hammil; age 49 years; occupation, farmer ; residence at Swanton, in election District No. 1, in Allegany county, Maryland, and have lived in Allegany county all my life.

By Mr. Spates :

Question. Were you registered as a voter prior to the election held in said Allegany county, on the 6th day of November, 1866?

Answer. I was.

By Mr. Spates :

Question. Did you or not attend at the polls in said election District, in Allegany county, on the 6th day of November, 1866, if so, did you then and there offer a ticket to the Judges of election at said polls as your ballot, and was it received or rejected ? State also the name of the person printed on said ticket, for State Senator, for whom you desired to vote, and what reason did the said Judges assign for rejecting your vote if they did so reject it ?

(Interrogatory objected to by Dr. Ohr.)

Answer. I did so attend and offered to the Judges of election there, a ticket as my ballot and it was rejected by them; the name on my said ticket for State Senator was Alfred

Spates; the reason assigned by said Judges for rejecting my vote, was that there were charges against me, and I did not vote.

By Alfred Spates :

Question, To which of the political parties did the Judges of election in District No. 1 belong and what are their names?

Answer. They belonged to the party called Radicals; their names are Samuel W. Friend, Ebenezer Kitzmiller and William W. Bray.

By A. Spates :

Question. Do you know any other matter or thing that would be of benefit to the contestant in this case?

Answer. I may say that the polls were held not at the usual place of holding the elections in that District.

Cross-Examined by Dr. Ohr.

By Dr. Ohr :

Question. When were you registered as a voter?

Answer. I was registered as a voter in 1866; I don't remember the precise date.

By Dr. Ohr :

Question. Did you apply for registration in 1865?

Answer. I did not.

By Dr. Ohr :

Question. Do you or not know that you had then been registered as disqualified for disloyalty?

(Question objected to by A. Spates.)

Answer. I did not know it in 1865 ; I knew it in 1866, when I applied for registration.

By Dr. Ohr.

Question. Did or did not the Judges of election in November, 1866, demand of you to take the oath prescribed in the Constitution, Article 1, section 4, before deciding upon your right to vote?

Answer. They did.

By Dr. Ohr :

Question. Did you or not decline to take said oath?

Answer. At first I did, but afterwards I did take said oath.

By Dr. Ohr :

Question. Did you after taking said oath, tender your ballot to the said Judges and was it then rejected by them?

Answer. I did not.

By Dr. Ohr :

Question. Was notice of the place of holding said election posted or given by the Sheriff or by his authority ; and was the election held at the place designated in said notice?

Answer. I do not know.

P. HAMILL.

Deposition No. 2.

John Phillips, having been by me duly sworn, deposed and said as follows, to wit:

By Mr. Spates:

Question. What is your name, age, occupation and residence?

Answer. My name is John Phillips; age 52 years; occupation farmer; residence in District No. 10, in Allegany county, Maryland, and have lived there seven years.

By Mr. Spates:

Question. Were you registered as a voter prior to the election held in said Allegany county, on the 6th day of November, 1866?

Answer. I was.

By Mr. Spates:

Question. Did you or not attend at the polls in said Election District No. 10, in Allegany county, on the 6th day of November, 1866; if so, did you then and there offer a ticket to the Judges of Election at said polls as your ballot; and was it received or rejected; state also the name of the person for State Senator printed on said ticket, and for whom you desire to vote; and what reason did the said Judges assign for rejecting your vote, if they did so reject it?

(Objected to by Dr. Ohr.)

Answer. I did so attend and offered my ballot, and it was rejected by the Judges of Election peremptorily and immediately. Alfred Spates was the name of the person on my ballot, for whom I desired to vote for State Senator. The reason the Judges assigned for so rejecting my vote was that there were charges.

By Mr. Spates:

Question. To which of the political parties did the Judges of Election in District No. 10 belong, and what are their names?

Answer. They are Abolitionists, sir; their names are Jas. Chisholm, Sr., William Waltz and George S. Lee.

By Mr. Spates:

Question. Do you know any other matter or thing that would be of benefit to the contestant in this case?

Answer. I know there were many armed men there at the polls who intimidated other persons from offering their votes.

By Mr. Spates:

Question. To which of the two political parties did said armed men belong?

Answer. To the Abolitionists, or Radicals, as they are called.

By Mr. Spates:

4

Question. Was there a general attendance at the polls in said district on the day above named ; and did you or not see any registered voters there who did not offer to vote under the above circumstances of intimidation; if so, name them, and state if you know for whom they would have voted for State Senator had they not been thus intimidated, and to which political party they belonged ?

(Objected to by Dr. Ohr.)

Answer. There was a general attendance on said day, and I saw there registered voters who did not vote by reason of said intimidation. The name of one of them so intimidated is John Ridder, Jr., who would have voted for Alfred Spates for State Senator; said Ridder belonged to the Conservative party. I understood there were others who were so intimidated.

Cross-examined by Dr. Ohr.

By Dr. Ohr :
Question. When were you registered as a voter ?
Answer. In 1866.
By Dr. Ohr :
Question. Did you apply for registration in 1865 ?
Answer. I did not.
By Dr. Ohr :
Question. Do you or not know that you had then been registered as disqualified for disloyalty ?

(Question objected to by Mr. Spates.)

Answer. I did not know anything about it until I saw the books where I was registered in 1866.
By Dr. Ohr :
Question. Did or did not the Judges of Election, in November, 1866, demand of you to take the oath prescribed in the Constitution, Art. 1, sec. 4, before deciding upon your right to vote?
Answer. No, sir; it was an unconditional and peremptory refusal.
By Dr. Ohr :
Question. In your answer to interrogatory 5th of direct examination you stated there were a great many armed men at the polls who intimidated other persons from voting—name the armed persons and the arms you saw them have?
Answer. I saw Archibald Chisholm, Jr., with a rifle on his shoulder; the other parties, who had revolvers and rifles, I know by sight, but don't know their names.
By Mr. Ohr :
Question. Did you see or hear Mr. Archibald Chisholm, Jr., use any threats or violence towards any persons, and whom ?

Answer. I did not.

By Dr. Ohr :

Question. Is it not customary with many of your people to
carry their rifles to public gatherings; and have you not seen
them with their rifles and guns at former elections?

Answer. I have seen on former elections a few guns with
parties, but never saw such an armed display of small arms
and large arms at an election before. It was currently reported that they were coming there to carry the election by
force of arms.

By Mr. Ohr :

Question. By whom was it intended to carry the election
by arms; and from whom did you hear the report; and did
you hear any Abolitionists or Radicals say they so intended?

Answer. By the Radicals; the report came through my
family, the Hoyes. I did not hear any Radicals say so, for
I had no conversation with any of them politically.

By Dr. Ohr .

Question. To what party do your family, the Hoyes, belong?

Answer. To the Conservative party.

JOHN PHILLIPS.

Deposition No. 3.

Elliot C. Tabb, having been by me duly sworn, deposed
and said as follows, to wit:

By Mr. Spates .

Question. What is your name, age, occupation and residence, and how long have you resided there?

Answer. My name is Elliott C. Tabb, aged 40 years, occupation, farmer and grazier, and reside in Ryan's Glade District No. 10, in Allegany county, Maryland, for the last
even or eight years.

By Mr. Spates :

Question. Were you registered as a voter prior to the election held in said Allegany county, on the 6th day of November, 1866?

Answer. I was.

By Mr Spates :

Question. Did you or not attend at the polls in said Election District, in Allegany county, on the 6th day of November, 1866; if so, did you then and there offer a ticket to the
Judges of Election, at said polls, as your ballot and was it
received or rejected; state also the name of the person printed
on said ticket for State Senator, for whom you desired to vote;
and what reason did the said judges assign for rejecting your
vote, if they did so reject it?

(objected to by Dr. Ohr.)

Answer. I went to the polls on that day in Election District No. 10, where I was registered and offered my ballot, and it was rejected by the judges; I desired to vote for Alfred Spates for State Senator. The judges refused to take my vote unless I would take the oath again; I declined to take the oath, telling them I had been registered; I went away without voting.

I asked them why they asked me to take the oath again; had I not been registered by a Register appointed by the Governor of the State? one of the judges replied then, that " the reason why that had to be done was, that the Governor himself was disloyal, and had committed several disloyal acts; If he had been a loyal man, we would have had none of this to do;" these are, as well as I can recollect, his words.

By Mr. Spates:

Question. To which of the political parties did the Judges of Election in District No. 1 belong, and what are their names?

Answer. They belonged to the Radical party; their names are James Chisholm, Sr., George S. Lee and William Waltz.

By Mr. Spates:

Question: Do you know any other matter or thing that would be of benefit to the Contestant in this case?

Answer. When I went to the polls on that day, I saw a number of armed men there, more than I ever saw before at any election; some with pistols belted around them; some with guns and some with pistols and guns both.

By Mr. Spates.

Question. To which of the two political parties did said armed men belong?

Answer. They belonged to the Radical party; I saw one man there have a gun, who, I understood was a Conservative man.

Crsss-examined by Dr. Ohr.

By Dr. Ohr:
Question. When were you registered as a voter?
Answer. In 1866.
By Dr. Ohr:
Question. Did you apply for registration in 1865?
Answer. I did not.
By Dr. Ohr:
Question. Do you or do you not know that you had then been registered as disqualified for disloyalty.

(Objected to by Mr. Spates:)

Answer. I did not know until I went to be registerd in

1866; then I found I had not been registered at all; my name
was not on the book.

By Dr. Ohr :
Did or did not the Judges of Election in November, 1866,
demand of you to take the oath prescribed in the Constitution,
Art. 1, See. 4, before deciding upon your right to vote?

Answer. Yes sir, they wanted me to take that oath.

By Dr. Ohr :
Question. Did you or did you not decline to take that oath?

Answer. I did decline.

By Dr. Ohr:
Question. Name the armed men you saw, and the political
party or parties to which they belonged?

Answer. I saw Beckwith Shrout, Archibald Chisholm, Jr.,
John Chisholm, B. F. Harvey, Crampton Harvey, John W.
Irons, Benjamin Moon, who all were armed, some with pis-
tols, and some with guns, and belonged to the Radical party.
There were others whose names I do not recollect, and who I
am satisfied belonged to the Radical party.

I saw James Liller there with a gun, and I understood he
was a Conservative; I saw no other Conservatives there with
arms. I saw Liller, above named, standing out on the road,
the North-western Pike, talking to a crowd of men, standing
there away from where the Radicals were. I dont remember
that there was any noise in the crowd, only talking as men
usually talk at an election.

By. Dr. Ohr :
Question. Did you hear or see any persons using threats or
violence; if so, name them?

Answer. I did not, whilst I was there, it was as quiet and
peaceable as elections usually are; I was there only about
fifteen minutes.

E. C. TABB.

Deposition No. 4.

HENRY THOMPSON, having been by me duly affirmed, deposed and said, as follows, to wit:

By Mr. Spates:
Question. What is your name, age, occupation and residence? and how long have you resided there?

Answer. My name is Henry Thompson, age 46 years, occupation farmer, and reside in District No. 10, in Allegany
county, Maryland, for many years.

By Mr. Spates:
Question. Were you registered as a voter prior to the election held in said Allegany county, on the 6th day of November 1866?

Answer. I was.

By Mr. Spates:

Question. Did you or not attend at the polls, in said Election District, in Allegany county, on the 6th day of November 1866; If so, did you then and there offer a ticket to the Judges of election, at said polls, as your ballot, and was it received or rejected? State also the name of the person printed on said ticket for State Senator, for whom you desired to vote. And what reason did the said Judges assign for rejecting your vote, if they did so reject it?

(Objected to by Dr. Ohr.)

Answer. I did go the polls on said day, and offered my ballot to the Judges of Election and it was rejected; I intended to vote for Alfred Spates for State Senator.

I asked the Judges what they had against me, and they said they had nothing; they would not receive my ticket.

Cross-examined by Dr. Ohr.

By Dr. Ohr:
Question. When were you registered as a voter?
Answer. In 1866.
By Dr. Ohr:
Question. Did you apply for registration in 1865?
Answer; I did not.
By Dr. Ohr:
Question. Do you or not know that you had been registered as disqualified, for disloyalty?

(Objected to by Mr. Spates.)

Answer. I knew nothing about it until this Fall, when I saw my name there.
By Dr. Ohr:
Question. Did or did not the Judges of Election in November 1866, demand of you to take the oath prescribed in the Constitution, Art. 1, sec. 4, before deciding upon your right to vote?
Answer. They did not.

HENRY THOMPSON.

Deposition No. 5.

CHARLES BEST, having been by me duly sworn, deposed and said as follows, to wit:
By Mr. Spates:
Question. What is your name, age, occupation and residence; and how long have you resided there?
Answer. My name is Charles Best, age 54 years, occupation, school teacher, and reside in District No. 10, in Allegany county, Maryland, and have done so about twelve years.
By Mr. Spates:
Question. Were you registered as a voter prior to the elec-

tion held in said Allegany county, on the 6th November 1866?

Answer. I was.

By Mr. Spates:

Question. Did you or not attend at the polls in said Election District in Allegany county, on the 6th day of November 1866; If so, did you then and there offer a ticket to the Judges of election at said polls, as your vote, and was it received or rejected; state also the name of the person printed on said ticket, for State Senator, for whom you desired to vote and what reason did the said Judges assign for rejecting your vote, if they did so reject it?

(Objected to by Dr. Ohr.)

Answer. I did go to the polls on that day and offered my ballot to the Judges of election, and they refused to receive it; 1 intended to vote for Alfred Spates for State Senator.

When I asked them what reason they had for rejecting my vote, they said there were charges against me, I did not therefore vote.

Cross-examined by Dr. Ohr.

By Dr. Ohr:

Question. When were you registered as a voter?

Answer. In 1866.

By Dr. Ohr:

Question. Did you apply for registration in 1865?

Answer. I did not.

By Dr. Ohr:

Question. Do you or not know that you had then been registered as disqualified for disloyalty?

(Objected to by Mr. Spates,)

Answer. I did not.

By Dr. Ohr:

Question. Did or did not the Judges of election in November 1866, demand of you to take the oath prescribed in the Constitution, Article 1, section 4, before deciding upon your right to vote?

Answer. They did not or I would have done so.

CHARLES BEST.

Deposition No. 6.

FRANCIS MARTIN, having been by me duly sworn, deposed and said, as follows to wit:

By Mr. Spates:

Question. What is your name, age, occupation and residence; and how long have you resided there?

Answer. My name is Francis Martin, age 44 years, occupation farmer, and reside in District No. 10, in Allegany county, Maryland, and have done so for over thirty years.

By Mr. Spates:

Question. Were you registered as a voter prior to the election held in said Allegany county, on the 6th day of November 1866?

Answer. I was.

Question by Mr. Spates:

Did you or not attend at the polls in said election District in Allegany county, on the 6th day of November, 1866? If so, did you then and there offer a ticket to the judges of election at said polls, as your ballot, and was it received or rejected? State also, the name of the person printed on said ticket, for State Senator for whom you desired to vote; and what reason did the judges assign for rejecting your vote, if they did so reject it?

(Objected to by Dr. Ohr.)

Answer. I went to the polls on said day and offered my ballot to the judges of election, and they refused to take it. I intended to vote for Alfred Spates for State Senator. The reason they assigned for not taking my ballot was that I had to be sworn before them, the same as I was before the Register, and this I refused to do.

Cross-Examined by Dr. Ohr.

Question by Dr. Ohr:

When were you registered as a voter?

Answer. About the 11th of September, 1866.

Question by Dr. Ohr:

Did you apply for registration in 1865?

Answer. I did not.

Question by Dr. Ohr:

Do you or not know that you had then been registered as disqualified for loyalty?

(Objected to by Mr. Spates.)

Answer. I did not know it until I went to be registered in September, 1866, when I saw my name in the book thus: "Francis Martin, refused to take the oath."

his

FRANCIS ⋈ MARTIN.

mark.

Witness—Michael Fallon.

Deposition No. 7

Frederick P. Saucer having been by me duly sworn, deposed and said as follows, to wit:

Question by Mr. Spates ;
What is your name, age, occupation and residence ? and how long have you lived there ?

Answer. My name is Frederick P. Saucer, age 40 years, occupation farmer, and reside in Allegany county, in District No. 10, and have done so for seven years.

Question by Mr. Spates :
Were you registered as a voter prior to the election held in said Allegany county on the 6th day of November, 1866 ?

Answer. I was·

Question by Mr. Spates :
Did you or not attend at the polls in said election District in Allegany county, on the 6th day of November, 1866 ? If so, did you then and there offer a ticket to the judges of election at said polls, as your ballot, and was it ·received or rejected ? state also the name of the person printed on said ticket for State Senator, for whom yeu desired to vote ; and what reason did the said judges assign for rejecting your vote, if they did so reject it ?

(Objected to by Dr. Ohr.)

Answer. I did attend at the polls on said day and offered my ballot to the judges of election, and it was rejected by them. I intended to vote then for Alfred Spates for State Senator. They said it was law for to swear me. I told them I had been registered, and that one oath was as good as a dozen. I did not vote.

Cross-examined by Dr. Ohr.

By Dr. Ohr.
Question. When were you registered as a voter ?
Answer. In 1866.
By Dr. Ohr.
Question. Did you apply for registration in 1865 ?
Answer. I did not.
By Dr. Ohr.
Question. Do you or not know that you had then been registered as disqualified for disloyalty ?

'(Objected to by Mr. Spates.)

Answer. I do not.

FREDERICK P. SAUCER.

Deposition No. 8.

George L. Mosser, having been by me duly sworn, deposed and said as follows, to wit :

By Mr. Spates.
Question. What is your name, age, occupation and residence ; and how long have you resided there ?

5

Answer. My name is George L. Mosser, age 40 years, occupation farmer, and reside in election District No. 10, in Allegany county, Maryland, and have done so since 1840.

By Mr. Spates.

Question. Were you registered as a voter prior to the election held in said Allegany county on the 6th November, 1866?

Answer. I was.

By Mr. Spates.

Question. Did you or not attend at the polls in said election District, in Allegany county on the 6th of November 1866; if so, did you then and there offer a ticket to the judges of election at said polls, as your ballot, and was it received or rejected? state also the name of the person printed on said ticket for State Senator, for whom you desired to vote? And what reason did the said judges assign for rejecting your vote, if they did so reject it?

(Objected to by Dr. Ohr.)

Answer. I did attend the polls that day, and offered my ballot to the judges of election, and they refused to receive it. I wanted to vote for Alfred Spates, for State Senator, whose name was on my ticket. The judges wanted me to take the oath, and I would not do it. I was sworn twice before.

Cross-examined by Dr. Ohr.

By Dr. Ohr:

Question. When were you registered as a voter?

Answer. In 1866.

By Mr. Ohr:

Question. Did you apply for registration in 1865?

Answer. I did not—I knew nothing of it, until it was too late.

By Dr. Ohr:

Question. Do you or not know that you had been registered as disqualified for disloyalty?

Answer. I did not.

By Dr. Ohr:

Question. You said in your answer to the 3d interrogatory-in-chief, that you had been sworn twice before; on what occasions, for what purpose and by whom?

Answer. When I was registered, I swore once—and once I swore before the military, to support the Constitution when they had arrested me.

GEORGE L. MOSSER.

Deposition No. 9.

DAVID E. HAUSER, having been by me duly sworn, deposed and said as follows, to wit:

By Mr. Spates:

Question. What is your name, age, occupation and residence, and how long have you lived there?

Answer. My name is David E. Hauser, age 35 years, occupation farmer, and reside in Election District No. 10, in Allegany county, Maryland, and have lived there since I was born.

By Mr. Spates:

Question. Were you registered as a voter prior to the election held in Allegany county on the 6th November, 1866?

Answer. I was.

By Mr. Spates:

Question. Did you or not attend at the polls in said Election District, in Allegany county, on the 6th day of November, 1866; if so, did you then and there offer a ticket to the Judges of Election at said polls, as your vote, and was it received or rejected; state also the name of the person printed on said ticket for State Senator, for whom you desired to vote; and what reason did the said Judges assign for rejecting your vote, if they did so reject it?

(Objected to by Dr. Ohr.)

Answer. I went to the polls on said day and offered my ballot to the Judges of Election, and they refused to take it; my ticket had on it for State Senator, the name of Alfred Spates. The judges assigned no reasons, but refused to take my ballot.

Cross-examined by Dr. Ohr.

By Dr. Ohr.

Question. When were you registered as a voter?
Answer. In 1866; this last Fall.

By Mr. Ohr:

Question. Did you apply for registration in 1865?
Answer. I did not.

By Dr. Ohr:

Question. Do you or not know that you had then been registered as disqualified for disloyalty?

(Objected to by Mr. Spates.)

Answer. I do not.

By Dr. Ohr:

Question. Did or did not the Judges of Election in November, 1866, demand of you to take the oath prescribed in the Constitution, Article 1, section 4, before deciding upon your right to vote?

Answer. They did; but I refused to do so.

DAVID E. HAUSER.

Deposition No. 10.

JACOB P. GAUER, having been by me duly sworn, deposed and said as follows, to wit:

By Mr. Spates:

Question. What is your name, age, occupation and residence, and how long have you resided there?

Answer. My name is Jocob P. Gauer, age 27 years, occupation, farming; and reside in Election District No. 10, in Allegany county, Maryland, and have lived there all my life.

By Mr. Spates:

Question. Were you registered as a voter prior to the election held in said Allegany county, on the 6th day of November, 1866?

Answer. I was.

By Mr. Spates:

Question. Did you or not attend at the polls in said Election District on the 6th day of November, 1866; if so, did you then and there offer a ticket to the Judges of Election at said polls, as your ballot, and was it received or rejected; state also the name of the person printed on said ticket for State Senator, for whom you desired to vote; and what reason did the said judges assign for rejecting your vote, if they did so reject it?

(Objected to by Mr. Ohr.)

Answer. I went to the polls on that day and offered my ballot to the Judges of Election, and they refused to receive it; by ticket had on it the name of Alfred Spates, for State Senator. They wanted me to take the oath over again, I asked them to read it to me, they did so, and as I had already taked that oath, I declined to do so, and they refused. my ballot.

Cross-examined by Dr. Ohr.

By Dr. Ohr:

Question. When were you registered as a voter?

Answer. In the Fall of 1866.

By Dr. Ohr:

Question. Did you apply for registration in 1865?

Answer. I did not.

By Dr. Ohr:

Question. Do you or not know that you had then been registered as disqualified for disloyalty?

(Objected to by Mr. Spates.)

Answer. No sir; my name was not on the books at all.

JACOB P. GAUER.

Deposition No. 11

HENRY HAMILL, having been by me duly sworn and examined, deposed and said as follows:

By Mr. Spates:

Question. What is your name, age, occupation and residence?

Answer. My name is Henry Hamill, age 68 years, occupation, farming, and reside in Election District No. 1, in Allegany county, Maryland, and have lived in Allegany county forty-five years.

By Mr. Spates:

Question. Were you registered as a voter prior to the election held in Allegany county, on the 6th of November, 1866?

Answer. I was.

By Mr. Spates.

Question. Did you or not attend at the polls in said Election District, in Allegany county, on the 6th day of November, 1866, if so did you then and there offer a ticket to the Judges of Election at said polls, as your ballot, and was it received or rejected, state also, the name of the person printed on said ticket for State Senator, for whom you desired to vote. and what reason did the said Judges assign for rejecting your vote, if they did so reject it?

(Objected to by Dr. Ohr.)

Answer. I went to the polls on that day to vote, and offered my ballot to the Judges of Election and they rejected it; My ticket had on it, for State Senator, the name of Alfred Spates; they gave me no reason, they said I was challenged, I asked who challenged me, they said they did not know, they then held a consultation in one corner of the room, in which the polls were held, and I asked them to decide, they came forward and said they had decided against me; I asked upon what ground, and one of them pointing to the papers on the table, said, upon that there; I asked them what that was, the reply was, "I don't know."

Cross-examined by Dr. Ohr.

By Dr. Ohr:

Question. When were you registered as a voter?

Answer. In 1866, sometime in September.

By Dr. Ohr:

Question. Did you apply for registration in 1865?

Answer. I did not sir.

By Dr. Ohr:

Question. Do you or not, know that you had then been registered as disqualified for disloyalty?

(Objected to by Mr. Spates.)

Answer. I know that my name was put there as disloyal.

By Dr. Ohr:

Question. Did or did not the Judges of Election in Nov., 1866, demanded of you to take the oath prescribed in the Constitution, Article 1, section 4, before deciding upon your right to vote?

Answer. They did not.

HENRY HAMMIL.

Deposition No. 12.

J. McCLURE MASON, having been by me duly sworn, deposed and said as follows, to wit:

By Mr. Spates:

Question. What is your name, age, occupation and residence, and how long have you lived there?

Answer. My name is J. McClure Mason, age 50 years, occupation, farming, and reside in Election District No. 10, in Allegany county, Maryland, and have lived there twenty-two years.

By Mr. Spates:

Question. Were you registered as a voter prior to the election held in said Allegany county on the 6th day of November, 1866?

Answer. I was.

By Mr. Spates:

Question. Did you or not, attend at the polls in said Election District, on the 6th day of November 1866, if so did you then and there offer a ticket to the Judges of Election at said polls as your ballot, and was it received or rejected, state also the name of the person printed on said ticket for State Senator, for whom you desired to vote, and what reason did the said judges assign for rejecting your vote, if they did so reject it?

(This question objected to by Dr. Ohr, in each case, throughout this examination.)

Answer. I went to the polls on said day and offered my ballot to the Judges of Election in said District, and they refused to receive it; the name of Alfred Spates for State Senator, was printed on my ticket so offered; the judges gave me no reason for rejecting my vote; I asked them if all three of them had decided to reject it, and they said yes.

Cross-examined by Dr. Ohr.

By Dr. Ohr:

Question. When were you registered as a voter?

Answer. In September, 1866.

By Dr. Ohr :
Question. Did you apply for registration in 1865 ?
Answer. I did not.
By Dr. Ohr :
Question. Did you not know that you had then been regis-
tered as disqualified for disloyalty ?

(This question objected to by Mr. Spates in every case in
this examination.)

Answer. I did not know it.
By Dr. Ohr :
Question. Did or did not the Judges of Election in Novem-
ber, 1866, demand of you to take the oath prescribed in the
Constitution, Article 1, section 4, before deciding upon your
right to vote?
Answer. They did not.

J. McCLURE MASON.

Deposition No. 13.

A. C. HAMILL, being by me duly sworn, deposed and said
as follows, to wit:
By Mr. Spates:
Question. What is your name, age, occupation and resi-
dence, and how long have you lived there?
Answer. My name is A. C. Hammil, age 30 years, occupa-
tion, farmer, and live in Election District No. 1, in Allegany
county, Maryland, and have lived there all my life.
Question by Mr. Spates :
Were you registered as a voter prior to the election held in
Allegany county, on the 6th November, 1866?
Answer. I was.
Question by Mr. Spates :
Did you or not attend at the polls in said election district
on the said 6th November, 1866; if so, did you then and there
offer a ticket to the Judges of election, at said polls, as your ballot, and was it received or rejected? state also the name of
the person printed on said ticket for State Senator, for whom
you desired to vote; and what reason did the said Judges
assign for rejecting your vote, if they did so reject it?
Answer. I went to the polls, in said district, on said day,
and offered my ballot to the Judges of Election, and they
refused to take it; my ballot so offered had on it the name of
Alfred Spates for State Senator; the reason they assigned for
rejecting my vote was, that I was challenged. I asked who
challenged me; they told me they did not know; I asked
them what the challenge was, and they told me they did not
know; they refused to let me vote unless I would take an
oath, or the oath; they did not tell me what kind of oath it
was they wanted me to take; I refused to take it.

Cross-examined by Mr. Ohr.

Question by Dr. Ohr:

When were you registered as a voter?

Answer. In August, 1866, I think.

Question by Dr. Ohr:

Did you apply for registration in 1865?

Answer. I did not.

Question by Dr. Ohr:

Do you or not know that you had then been registered as disqualified for disloyalty?

Answer. No, sir, I did not.

Question by Dr. Ohr:

Did or did not the Judges of Election in November, 1866, demand of you to take the oath prescribed in the Constitution, Article 1, section 4, before deciding upon your right to vote?

Answer. They required of me take the oath, or an oath— whether it was that oath or not, I can't say, for they did not tell me.

A. C. HAMMIL.

Deposition No. 14.

JOHN J. WHIRREL, having been by me duly sworn, deposed and said as follows, to wit:

By Mr. Spates:

Question. What is your name, age, occupation and residence, and how long have you lived there?

Answer. My name is John James Whirrel, age, 23 years, occupation farmer, and live in Election District No. 10, Allegany county, Maryland, and have lived there twenty years,

Question by Mr. Spates;

Were you registered as a voter prior to the election held in said Allegany county, on the 6th of November, 1866?

Answer. I was.

Question by Mr. Spates:

Did you or not attend at the polls in said election district on the 6th November, 1866; and if so, did you then and there offer a ticket to the Judges of Election at said polls as your ballot, and was it received or rejected; state also the name of the person printed on said ticket for State Senator, for whom you desired to vote; and what reason did the said Judges assign for rejecting your vote, if they did so reject it?

Answer. I went to the polls in that district on said day and offered my ballot to the Judges of Election, and they refused to receive it. My ballot had on it for State Senator the name of Alfred Spates. The reason the Judges assigned for refusing my vote was, that I had said in 1865 that I thought the

South was right. One of the Judges said he heard me say so.

Cross-examination by Dr. Ohr.

Question by Dr. Ohr :

Did the Judges of Election demand of you to take the oath prescribed in Article 1, section 4, of the Constitution, before deciding on your right to vote ?

Answer. They did not.

his
JOHN J. WHIRREL.
mark

Witness.—M. FALLON.

Deposition No. 15.

WILLIAM ARNOLD, having by me been duly sworn, deposed and said as follows, to wit ;

Question by Mr. Spates.

What is your name, age, occupation and residence, and how long have you resided there?

Answer. My name is William Arnold, age 36 years, occupation farming, and reside in Election District No. 10 in Allegany county, Maryland, and have lived there all my life.

Question by Mr. Spates:

Were you registered as a voter prior to the election held in said county, on the 6th November, 1866 ?

Answer. I was.

Question by Mr. Spates :

Did you or not attend at the polls in said election district on the 6th day of November, 1866 ; if so, did you then and there offer a ticket to the Judges of Election at said polls as your ballot, and was it received or rejected ; state, also, the name of the person printed on said ticket for State Senator for whom you desired to vote ; and what reason did the said Judges assign for rejecting your vote, if they did so reject it ?

Answer. I went to the polls in my District, on said day, and could not get to the window, on account of the crowd there, there were armed men standing there on one end of the porch and men coming in on the other. I saw there many good Constitutional men, who could not get to vote ; their tickets being refused by the Judges, and I therefore turned off and went home without voting; The name of Alfred Spates for State Senator, was printed on the ticket I had and wished to vote.

Cross-examined by Dr. Ohr.

By Dr. Ohr :

Question. When were you registered as a voter ?

6

Answer. In September, 1866.
By Dr. Ohr:
Question. Did you apply for registration in 1865 ?
Answer. I did not.
By Dr. Ohr:
Question. Did you or not know that you had then been registered as disqualified for disloyalty ?
Answer. I do not know.
By Dr. Ohr:
Question. Did you offer your ballot to the Judges?
Answer. I did not.

WILLIAM ARNOLD.

Deposition No. 16.

GEORGE H. O'BRIEN, having been by me duly sworn, deposed and said as follows :
By Mr. Spates.
Question. What is your name, age, occupation and residence, and how long have you lived there?
Answer. My name is George H. O'Brien; age 30 years; occupation farming, and reside in District No. 1, in Allegany county, Maryland, and have lived there five years.
By Mr. Spates :
Question. Where you registered as a voter prior to the election held in said county, on the 6th of November, 1866 ?
Answer. I was.
By Mr. Spates :
Question. Did you or not attend at the polls in said electtion District, in Allegany county, on the 6th day of November, 1866; if so, did you then and there offer a ticket to the Judges of election at said polls as your ballot, and was it received or rejected? state also the name of the person printed on said ticket for State Senator, for whom you desired to vote, and what reason did the said Judges assign for rejecting your vote, if they did so reject it?
Answer. I attended at the polls in my District on that day and offered my ballot to the Judges, and they all refused to take it and allow me to vote ; the name of Alfred Spates for States Senator, was on the ticket I had and offered to the Judges when I wanted to vote that day; the reasons assigned by the Judges for refusing my vote was that Mr. Friend, one of the Judges, said I had given a horse to Mr. West to go South, which I now say I did not do; I offered my vote to all of them and each of them refused it. Another reason assigned by the Judges, was that I had given Charley West and Hiram Taskar, something to eat after they had been South.

Cross-examined by Dr. Ohr.

By Dr. Ohr:
Question. When were you registered as a voter ?
Answer. In September, 1866.
By Mr. Ohr:
Question. Did you apply for registration in 1865?
Answer I did not.
By Dr. Ohr:
Question. Do you or not know that you had then been registered as disqualified for disloyalty ?
Answer. No, sir, I don't.
By Mr. Ohr;
Question. Did or did not the Judges of election in November, 1866, demand of you to take the oath prescribed in the Constitution, Article 1, section 4, before deciding upon your right to vote ?
Answer. They did not.

GEORGE H. O'BRIEN.

Deposition No. 17.

DAVID S. ARNOLD, having been by me duly sworn, deposed and said as follows, to wit :
By Mr. Spates :
Question. What is your name age, occupation and residence and how long have you resided there?
Answer. My name is David S. Arnold; age 38; occupation farmer, and reside in election District No. 10, in Allegany county Maryland, and have lived there all my life time.
By Mr. Spates :
Question. Where you registered as a voter prior to the election held in Allegany county, November 6, 1866?
Answer. I was registered the 11th September, 1866.
By Mr. Spates :
Question. Did you or not attend at the polls in said election District, on the 6th day of November, 1866 ; if so, did you then and there offer a ticket to the Judges of election at said polls as your ballot, and was it received or rejected; state also the name of the person printed on said ticket for State Senator for whom you desired to vote ; and what reason did the said Judges assign for rejecting your vote, if they did so reject it ?
Answer. I did so attend and offered my ballot to the Judges of election, and it was rejected by them; the name of Alfred Spates for State Senator, was printed on the ticket I desired to vote, and offered to the Judges of election ; the Judges told me at the time that I could not vote.

₃

Cross-examined by Dr. Ohr.

By Dr. Ohr:
Question. Did or did not the Judges of Election in November, 1866, demand of you to take the oath prescribed in the Constitution, Art. 1, sec. 4, before deciding upon your right to vote?
Answer. They did not.
By Dr. Ohr:
Question. Did the Judges tell you why you could not vote?
Answer. They did not—they assigned no reason.
By Dr. Ohr:
Question. Do you or do you not know that you had been registered for disloyalty in 1865?
Answer. I do not, sir.

DAVID S. ARNOLD.

Deposition No. 18.

WILLIAM H. KITZMILLER, having been by me duly sworn, deposed and said as follows, to wit:
By Mr. Spates:
Question. What is your name, age, occupation and residence, and how long have you lived there?
Answer. My name is William H. Kitzmiller; age 34 years; occupation shoemaker, and reside in Election District No. 10, in Allegany county, Maryland, and have lived there twelve years.
By Mr. Spates:
Question. Were you registered as a voter prior to the election held in said Allegany county, on the 6th of November, 1866?
Answer. I was registered on the 11th of September, 1866.
By Mr. Spates:
Question. Did you or not attend at the polls in said Election District, in Allegany county, on the 6th day of November, 1866; if so, did you then and there offer a ticket to the Judges of Election at said polls as your ballot, and was it received or rejected; state also the name of the person printed on said ticket for State Senator, for whom you desired to vote; and what reason did the said Judges assign for rejecting your vote, if they did so reject it?
Answer. I did so attend on the day and at the place named, and offered my ballot to the Judges of Election, and they refused to receive it. The name of Col. Alfred Spates was printed on the ticket I so offered and desired to vote, for State Senator. The Judges did not assign any particular reason; but said I could not vote there. This was my place to vote, and I had voted there before, in 1864, in the Spring, in April.

Cross-Examined by Dr. Ohr.

By Dr. Ohr.

Question. Why did the Judges say you could not vote there?

Answer. They said there were witnesses againt me—that I was disloyal.

By Dr. Ohr:

Question. Do you or do you not know that you had then been registered as disqualified for disloyalty?

Answer. I know that I saw my name on the registration book with the word "disloyal" after it; this was in 1866, when I was registered. I never applied to be registered until September, 1866.

By Mr. Spates:

Question. What efforts, it any, did you make to obtain your vote after the Judges had refused it, as detailed above?

Answer. I then called again upon them and insisted upon knowing their reasons why I should not vote. When they answered they said, "there was a witness against me who said I was guilty of piloting Rebels." I brought the witness they named to the door of the room in which the Judges were. I called to the Judges for admission, and they answered that the door was bolted. I then went to the window where the Judges were and they refused to admit me, after I had asked them to let me in with my witness, Alexander Kitzmiller, to disprove the charge against me. I told them I had Alexander Kitzmiller there to disprove the charges they had against me. Alexander Kitzmiller was the witness they named as the one making the charge against me of piloting the Rebels. The reason I took Kitzmiller with me to the Judges was, that he told me there that he had not made any such charge, and would go before them and swear that he did not make any such charge. When I went to the door of the room where the polls were held it was guarded by two armed men, John Chisholm and Beckwith Shrout, who both belonged to the Radical party. When I failed to get before the Judges I left without voting.

WILLIAM H. KITZMILLER.

Deposition No. 19.

JACOB SHAFFER, having been by me duly sworn, deposed and said as follows, to wit:

By Mr. Spates:

Question. What is your name, age, occupation and residence, and how long have you resided there?

Answer. My name is Jacob Shaffer; age 63 years; occupation wheelwright, and reside in Election District No. 10, in Allegany county, Maryland, and have lived there for the last three years and a half.

By Mr. Spates :

Question. Were you registered as a voter prior to the election held in Allegany county, November 6, 1866 ?

Answer. I was. I was registered in September, 1866.

By Mr. Spates :

Question. Did you or not attend at the polls in said Election District, in Allegany county, on the 6th day of November, 1866; if so, did you then and there offer a ticket to the Judges of Election at said polls as your ballot, and was it received or rejected; state also the name of the person printed on said ticket for State Senator, for whom you desired to vote; and what reason did the said Judges assign for rejecting your vote, if they did so reject it ?

Answer. I did attend at the polls on the day named, and offered my ticket at the window, and called to the Judges to receive my ticket, and they refused to take it. The ticket had on it the name of Mr. Alfred Spates, for Senator. The reason they assigned for rejecting my vote was, that in Virginia, before the war, I had voted for the ordinance of secession.

Cross-examined by Dr. Ohr.

By Dr. Ohr :

Question. Do you or do you not know that you had been registered as disqualified for disloyalty ?

(Objected to by Mr. Spates.)

Answer. When I went to be registered in September, 1866, I saw my name on the book with the word "disloyal" after it. I did not apply to be registered until September, 1866·

JACOB SHAFFER.

Deposition No. 20.

John A. Gauer, having been by me duly sworn, deposed and said as follows, to wit.

By Mr. Spates:

Question. What is your name, age, occupation and residence, and how long have you resided there?

Answer. My name is John A Gauer, age 31 years, occupation, shoemaker, and reside in Election District No. 10, in Allegany county, Maryland, and have lived there all my life time.

By Mr. Spates:

Question. Were you registered as a voter prior to the election held in said Allegany county, November 6th, 1866?

Answer. I was registered in September, 1866.

By Mr. Spates.

Question. Did you or not attend at the polls in said Election District, in Allegany county, on the 6th day of November, 1866; if so, did you then and there offer a ticket to the judges of election, at said polls as your ballot, and was it received or rejected; state also the name of the person printed on said ticket for State Senator, for whom you desired to vote; and what reason did the said judges assign for rejecting your vote, if they did so reject it?

Answer. I attended the polls on that day in District No. 10, I did not offer my ticket to the judges of election, because I saw others go up to vote, that were objected to and who did not get their votes. These parties did not get their votes because they refused to take the oath required of them by the judges of election; and I would not take the oath and therefore did not offer my vote. The name of Alfred Spates was printed on the ticket that I desired to vote, for State Senator.

By Mr. Spates:

Question. Was there or not a rule adopted by the judges of election in District No. 10, and announced to and known by persons generally in said district, that no one should vote without taking the oath before the said judges, who had been registered in 1866.

Answer. My father told me there was such a rule, and that is the reason I did not offer my vote.

his
JOHN A. ⋈ GAUER.
mark.

Attest—J. W. STRONG.

Deposition No. 21.

William Moon, having been by me duly sworn, deposed and said as follows, to wit:

By Mr. Spates:

Question. What is your name, age, occupation and residence, and how long have you lived there?

Answer. My name is William Moon, age 53 years, occupation farmer, reside in Election District No. 10, in Allegany county, Maryland, and have done so all my life time.

By Mr. Spates:

Question. Were you registered as a voter prior to the election in Allegany county, November 6th, 1866?

Answer. I was registered in September, 1866.

By Mr. Spates:

Question. Did you or not attend at the polls in said Election District in Allegany county, on the 6th day of November, 1866; if so, did you then and there offer a ticket to the judges of election at said polls, as your ballot, and was it received or rejected; state also the name of the person printed on said ticket for State Senator, for whom you desired to vote; and what reason did the said judges assign for rejecting your vote, if they did so reject it?

Answer. I did attend on that day at the polls and offered my ballot to the judges of election there, and they refused to receive it; the name of Alfred Spates, for State Senator, was printed on my ticket so offered. The judges assigned no reason at all, for refusing or rejecting my vote.

Cross-examined by Mr. Dr. Ohr.

By Dr. Ohr:

Question. Did or did not the judges of election in November, 1866, demand of you to take the oath prescribed in the Constitution, Art. 1, Sec. 4, before deciding upon your right to vote?

Answer. They did not, they merely said, I could not vote?

WILLIAM MOON.

Deposition No. 22.

John Ridder, Sr., having been by me duly sworn, deposed and said as follows, to wit.

By Mr. Spates:

Question. What is your name, age, occupation and residence, and how long have you live there?

Answer. My name is John Ridder, Sr., age, 68 years, occupation, farmer, and reside in Election District No. 10., in Allegany county, Maryland, and have lived there thirty years.

By Mr. Spates:

Question. Were you or not registered as a voter prior to the election held in Allegany county, on the 6th November, 1866?

Answer. I was registered in September, 1866.

By Mr. Spates:

Question. Did you or not attend at the polls in said Election District in Allegany county, on the 6th day of November, 186 ; if so, did you then and there offer a ticket to the judges of election at said polls, as your ballot, and was it received or rejected; state also, the name of the person printed on said ticket for State Senator, for whom you desired to vote; and what reason did the said judges assign for rejecting your vote, if they did so reject it?

Answer. I went to the polls on that day, and offered my ticket to the Judges of Election twice, and they said nothing, but refused to take it; the name on the ticket I offered, was Alfred Spates for State Senator.

Cross-examined by Dr. Ohr.

By Dr. Ohr:

Did or did not the Judges of Election, in November, 1866, demand of you to take the oath prescribed in the Constitution, Article 1, section 4, before deciding upon your right to vote?

Answer. No, sir : they did not ; they would not listen to me.

JOHN RIDER.

Deposition No. 23.

GEORGE H. GAUER, having been by me duly sworn, deposed and said as follows, to wit :

By Mr. Spates :

Question. What is your name, age, occupation and residence; and how long have you lived there?

Answer. My name is George H. Gauer, age 21 years; occupation, farmer ; and I live in election District No. 10, in Allegany county, Maryland, and I have lived there ever since I was born.

By Mr. Spates :

Question. Were you registered as a voter prior to the election held in Allegany county, November, 6th, 1866?

Answer I was, in September, 1866.

By Mr. Spates :

Question. Did you or not attend at the polls in said election District, in Allegany county, on the 6th day of November, 1866, if so, did you then and there offer a ticket to the Judges of election at said polls as your ballot, and was it received or rejected ? state also the name of the person printed on said ticket, for State Senator, for whom you desired to vote, and what reason did the said Judges assign for rejecting your vote if they did so reject it ?

Answer. I went to the polls on that day in my district, and offered my ticket to vote to the Judges of Election, and they refused to take it; the name printed on my ticket for State Senator which I desired to vote and offered, was Alfred Spates ; the Judges said if I would take the oath over again, I could vote, and if not, I could not vote ; I refused to take the oath then.

Cross-examination by Dr. Ohr.

By Dr. Ohr:

Question. Did you take any oath before the Judges of Election.

Answer. I did not ; I was born in August, and was just 21 when I was registered.

GEORGE H. GAUER.

Deposition No. 24.

DAVID A. GAUER, having been by me duly sworn, deposed and said as follows, to wit :

7

Question by Mr. Spates:
What is your name, age, occupation and residence, and how long have you lived there?
Answer. My name is David A. Gauer, age 21 years in March, 1866, occupation farmer, and live in Election District No. 10, in Allegany county, Maryland, and have lived there ever since I was born.
Question by Mr. Spates:
Were you registered as a voter prior to the election held in said county on the 6th day of November, 1866?
Answer. I was; in September, 1866.
Question by Mr. Spates:
Did you or not attend at the polls in said election district in Allegany county on the 6th day of November, 1866; if so, did you then and there offer a ticket to the Judges of Election at said polls as your ballot, and was it received or rejected; state also the name of the person printed on said ticket for State Senator, for whom you desired to vote; and what reason did the said Judges assign for rejecting your vote, if they did so reject it.
Answer. I attended at the polls on that day, and I offered a ticket as my ballot to the Judges of Election, and it was refused by them. The name printed on my ticket so offered was Alfred Spates, for State Senator; the Judges did not assign any reason for refusing my vote.

Cross-examined by Dr. Ohr.

By Dr. Ohr:
Did or did not the Judges of Election, in November, 1866, demand of you to take the oath prescribed in the Constitution, Article 1, section 4, before deciding upon your right to vote?
Answer. I offered my ticket at the window where votes were taken, and they told me to come around inside into the house; and I refused to do so, saying, if they could not take it there, they could not take it inside; they refused to take it, and I went away without voting; they did not say why they wanted me inside.

his
DAVID A. GAUER.
mark

Witness.—PETER KNEPP.

Deposition No. 25.

Question by Mr. Spates:
What is your name, age, occupation and residence, and how long have you lived there?
Answer. My name is Peter Knepp, age 34 years, occupation farmer, and live in District No. 10 in Allegany county, Maryland, and have lived there for the last eight years.

Question by Mr. Spates :
Were you registered as a voter prior to the election held in
Allegany county, on the 6th day of. November, 1866 ?
Answer. I was ; in September, I think, 1866.
Question by Mr. Spates :
Did you or not attend at the polls in said election district
in Allegany county on the 6th day of November, 1866 ; if so,
did you then and there offer a ticket to the Judges of Election at said polls, as your ballot, and was it received or rejected ; state also the name of the person printed on said ticket
for State Senator, for whom you desired to vote ; and what
reason did the said Judges assign for rejecting your vote, if
they did so reject it?
Answer. I attended at the polls in said District on said
day; I offered my ballot then to the Judges of election and
they refused to take it The name on my ticket so offered,
for State Senator, was Alfred Spates.
The Judges assigned no reason at all for rejecting my
vote.

Cross-examined by Dr. Ohr.

By Dr. Ohr :
Question. Did or did not the Judges of election in Novem
ber 1866, demand of you to take the oath prescribed in the
Constitution, Article 1, section 4, before deciding upon your
right to vote?
Answer. No sir, they did not.
By Dr. Ohr :
Question. Do you or do you not know whether your name
was entered on the book of registration, and marked as "dis-
loyal," in 1865 ?
Answer. I do not know.
By Dr. Ohr :
Question. Did the Judges ask you to take any oath, or do
any other thing, before they refused your vote ?
Answer. They did not.

PETER KNEPP.

Deposition No. 26.

CHARLES O. NETHKIN, having been by me duly sworn, deposed and said as follows, to wit:
By Mr. Spates :
Question. What is your name, age, occupation and residence,
and how long have you lived there ?
Answer. My name is Charles O. Nethkin, age 34 years,
occupation, farmer, and live in Election District No. 10, Allegany county, Maryland, and have lived there ever since I
was born.
By Mr. Spates :
Question. Were you or not registered as a voter prior to

the election held in Allegany county, on the 6th November 1866?

Answer. I was —— in the year 1866.

By Mr. Spates:

Question. Did you or not attend at the polls in said Election District, in Allegany county, on the 6th day of November 1866; If so, did you then and there offer a ticket to the Judges of election at said polls, as your ballot, and was it received or rejected?

State also the name of the person printed on said ticket for State Senator, for whom you desired to vote?

And what reason did the said Judges assign for rejecting your vote, if they did so reject it?

Answer. I did attend at the polls on said day, in said District; I offered then and there my ticket as a ballot to the Judges of election, and they refused to receive it. The name of Col. Alfred Spates, for State Senator, was printed on the ticket so offered by me. The Judges assigned no reason for rejecting my vote.

Cross-examined by Dr. Ohr:

By Dr. Ohr:

Question. Do you or do you not know whether your name was entered on the book of registration in 1865, and marked as disloyal?

Answer. No sir, my name was not put on the book until I was registered in the Fall of 1866.

By Dr. Ohr:

Question. Did the Judges ask you to take any oath or do any other thing before they refused your vote?

Answer. They did not.

CHARLES O. NETHKIN.

Deposition No. 27.

JOHN GAUER, having been by me duly sworn and examined, deposed and said as follows, to wit:

By Mr. Spates:

Question. What is your name, age, occupation and residence, and how long have you lived there?

Answer. My name is John Gauer, age 70 years, occupation, farmer, and live in Election District No. 10, in Allegany county, Maryland and have lived there for the last sixty years.

By Mr. Spates:

Question. Were you registered as a voter prior to the election held in Allegany county, November 6th, 1866?

Answer. Yes, in September 1866.

By Mr. Spates:

Question. Did you not attend at the polls in said Election

District in Allegany county, on the 6th day of November 1865; If so, did you then and there offer a ticket to the Judges of election at said polls, as your ballot, and was it received or rejected; state also the name of the person printed on said ticket, for State Senator, for whom you desired to vote; and what reason did the said Judges assign for rejecting your vote, if they did so reject it?

Answer. I attended at the polls that day in my Election District No. 10, and there offered a ticket as my ballot to the Judges of election, and it was rejected by them. The name on the ticket, for State Senator, so offered by me, was Col. Al'red Spates. The Judges said I should take the oath; and I would not do it; and they then refused to take my vote.

(*Cross-Examined by Dr. Ohr, declined.*)

JOHN GAUER.

Deposition No. 28.

JOHN BEARD, having been by me duly sworn, deposed and said as follows, to wit:

By Mr. Spates:

Question. What is your name, age, occupation and residence? and how long have you lived there?

Answer. My name is John Beard, age 55 years, occupation farmer, and I live in Election District No. 10, in Allegany county, Maryland, and have lived there about fifty years.

By Mr. Spates:

Question. Were you registered as a voter prior to the election held in Allegany county, on the 6th day of November 1866?

Answer. I was, in September 1866, at the Red House in District No. 10, aforesaid.

By. Mr. Spates:

Question. Did you or not attend at the polls in said Election District, in Allegany county, on the 6th day of November, 1866; if so, did you then and there offer a ticket to the Judges of Election at said polls, as your ballot, and was it received or rejected; state also, the name of the person printed on said ticket for State Senator, for whom you desired to vote; and what reason did the said judges assign for rejecting your vote, if they did so reject it?

Answer. I attended at the polls on said day in my district, and offered a ticket to the Judges of Election, and they refused to take my ballot so offered. The name on my ticket so offered, for State Senator, was Mr. Alfred Spates, for whom I desired to vote. The judges said I should be qualified over again, and should take the oath before them. I declined to take it, and they then refused to let me vote, and I left the polls.

JOHN BEARD,

Deposition No. 29.

ALEXANDER FAIRALL, having been by me duly sworn, deposed and said as follows, to wit:

By Mr. Spates:

Question. What is your name, age, occupation and residence, and how long have you lived there?

Answer. My name is Alexander Fairall, age 37 years, occupation, postmaster and agent of Baltimore and Ohio Rail Road, at Swanton, Allegany county, Maryland. I have been living in Allegany county eighteen years, and at Swanton about two years.

By Mr. Spates:

Question. Were you registered as a voter prior to the 6th day of November, 1866, when the election was held in Allegany county?

Answer. I was, in September, 1866.

By Mr. Spates:

Question. Did you or not attend at the polls in said Election District, in Allegany county, on the 6th day of November, 1866; if so, did you then and there offer a ticket to the Judges of Election at said polls, as your ballot, and was it received or rejected; state also, the name of the person printed on said ticket, for State Senator, for whom you desired to vote; and what reason did the judges assign for rejecting your vote, if they did so reject it?

Answer. I did attend at the polls in my district on said day, and I offered to the Judges of Election at that time a ticket as my ballot, and they refused to take it. The name printed on my ticket for State Senator, and for whom I desired to vote, was Alfred Spates. Mr. Friend, one of the judges, said, that my vote was challeged—I asked by whom. He said my name was on a list. He then commenced to read the Registry Law to me, I told him I had read it. He then said I must come in—take the oath and answer questions—which I declined to do; he did not say what the questions were, nor did he say I could then vote.

Cross-examined by Dr. Ohr.

By Dr. Ohr:

Question. Do you or do you not know that your name was entered on the books of registration and marked as disloyal, in 1865?

Answer. My name was entered there, as refusing to take the oath.

ALEXANDER FAIRALL.

Deposition No. 30.

JACOB GAUER, of A., having been by me duly sworn, deposed and said as follows, to wit:

By Mr. Spates:

Question. What is your name, age, occupation and residence and how long have you lived there?

Answer. My name is Jacob Gauer, of A., age 46 years, occupation farmer, and live in Election District No. 10, in Allegany county, Maryland, and have lived in said county 25 years, and in the District at least 16 years.

By Mr. Spates:

Question. Where you registered as a voter prior to the election held in Allegany county, Nov. 6th, 1866?

Answer. I was, in September, 1866, at the Red House, in District No. 10.

By Mr, Spates:

Question. Did you or not attend at the polls in said Election District, in Allegany county, on the 6th day of November, 1866; if so, did you then and there offer a ticket to the Judges of Election, at said polls, as your ballot, and was it received or rejected; state also the name of the person printed on said ticket for State Senator, for whom you desired to vote; and what reason did the said judges assign for rejecting your vote, if they did so reject it?

Answer. I attended at said polls on said day above named, and I there offered to the Judges of Election my ballot, and they refused to receive it. The name on the ticket I so offered, was Alfred Spates, for State Senator, for whom I intended to vote. At first they did not say why they rejected it, afterwards they said I must come in and take the oath before I could have my vote, I told them I would not do it, I swore once and registered. They would not then take my ticket. They had an armed guard around the door—and there were many men there armed. These armed men belonged to the Radical party, I knew their faces, but not their names, some of them were the Harveys, and one of the Irons, one Beckwick Schrout, also who were armed. There was one man there, a Conservative, who had a gun, but he did not take it up to the polls. I suppose I could have got in if I wished to go, but I did not wish to do so. The voting was done at the window, the voter standing outside.

Cross-examined by Mr. Ohr.

By Dr. Ohr:

Question. Do you or do you not know that your name was entered on the book of registration as disloyal, in 1865?

Answer. I do not know that it was.

By. Dr. Ohr.

Question. Did these armed men use any threats or violence towards any one?

Answer. No, sir, not that I saw.

his
JACOB ⏚ GAUER, of A.
mark.

Witness—David S. Arnold.

Deposition No. 31.

John Conneway, having been by me duly sworn, deposed and said as follows, to wit:

By Mr. Spates.

Question. What is your name, age, occupation and residence; and how long have you lived there?

Answer. My name is John Conneway, age 66 years, occupation farmer, and live in election District No. 10, Allegany county, Maryland, and have lived there 24 years.

By Mr. Spates.

Question. Were you registered as a voter prior to the election held in said county November 6th, 1866?

Answer. I was, in September, 1866, at the Red House in said District No. 10.

By Mr. Spates.

Question. Did you or not attend at the polls in said election District, in Allegany county, on the 6th day of November, 1866; If so, did you then and there offer a ticket to the judges of election at said polls as your ballot, and was it received or rejected? state also the name of the person printed on said ticket for State Senator, for whom you desired to vote? and what reason did the said judges assign for rejecting your vote, if they did so reject it?

Answer. I went to the polls in my District on that day and offered my ticket as a voter, to the judges of election, and they refused to receive it. The name of Alfred Spates, for State Senator, was on the ticket I offered to vote. The judges said I was disloyal and they could not take my vote. They refused to take my ballot and I did not vote.

Cross-examined by Dr. Ohr.

By Dr. Ohr,

Question. Do or do you not know whether your name was entered on the book of Registration, and marked as disloyal in 1865?

Answer. I know it now. I saw it when I was registered in September, 1865.

By Dr. Ohr.

Question. Did or did not the judges of election in November, 1866, demand of you to take the oath prescribed in the

Constitution, Article 1, Sec. 4, before deciding on your right to vote ?

Answer. They did. I refused to take it, and told them I was sworn once and that would do.

JOHN CONNEWAY.

Deposition No. 32.

George Mosser, having been by me duly sworn, deposed and said as follows, to wit :

By Mr. Spates.

Question. What is your name, age, occupation and residence, and how long have you resided there?

Answer. My name is George Mosser, age 70 years, occupation farmer, and reside in election District No. 10, in Allegany county, Maryland, and have lived there 25 years.

By Mr. Spates.

Question. Were you registered as a voter prior to the election held in Allegany county November 6th, 1866 ?

Answer. I was, in September, 1866, in the Red House, in District No. 10.

By Mr. Spates.

Question. Did you or not attend at the polls in said election District, in Allegany county, on the 6th day of November, 1866 ; if so, did you then and there offer a ticket to the judges of election at said polls, as your bollot, and was it received or rejected; state also the name of the person printed on said ticket, for State Senator, for whom you desired to vote ; and what reason did the said judges assign for rejecting your vote, if they did so reject it ?

Answer. I went to the polls in my District on the day of the election in November last ; I offered my ballot at the window and it was rejected by the judges. The name of Alfred Spates, as State Senator, was on the ticket I wished to vote and offered to the judges. The judges said I should swear before they would let me vote. I told them I had sworn once and was not going to swear again. They did not tell me what they wanted me to swear, only that I must, in order to vote.

GEORGE MOSSER.

Deposition No. 33.

John C. Nethken, having been by me duly sworn, deposed and said as follows, to wit :

By Mr Spates.

Question. What is your name, age, occupation and residence, and how long have you lived there ?

Answer. My name is John C. Nethken, age 36 years, occupation farm work, and reside in election District No. 10, in Allegany county, Maryland, and was born and raised there.

8

By Mr. Spates.

Question. Were you registered as a voter prior to the election in Allegany county, November 6th, 1866?

Answer. Yes, I was, in the fall of 1866, at Israel Thompson's, in District No. 10.

By Mr. Spates.

Question. Did you or not attend at the polls in said election District. in, Allegany county, on the 6th day of November, 1866 ! if so, did you then and there offer a ticket to the judges of election at said polls, as your ballot, and was it received or rejected ; state also the name of the person printed on said ticket, for State Senator, for whom you desired to vote ; and what reason did the said judges assign for rejecting your vote, if they did so reject it ?

Answer. I did attend at the polls in my District, on said day, and offered a ticket as my ballot, to the judges of election at the polls, and they refused to receive it ; the name of Alfred Spates, for State Senator, was printed on the ticket I so offered and wished to vote. The judges said they could not take my vote unless I would take the oath. I refused to do so, and they refused to take my vote.

his
JOHN C. ⋈ NETHKEN.
mark.

Witness—J. M. Strong.

Deposition No. 34.

HENRY O. HAMILL, having been by me duly sworn, deposed and said as follows, to wit:

By Mr. Spates :

Question. What is your name, age, occupation and residence, and how long have you lived there?

Answer. My name is Henry O. Hamill, age 50 years, occupation, carpenter, and I reside in Election District No. 1, in Allegany county, Maryland, and have lived in the county all my lifetime, except about six years, and in District No. 1, two years last November.

By Mr. Spates :

Question. Were you registered as a voter prior to the election held in Allegany county, November 6th, 1866?

Answer. I was, in September, 1866.

By Mr. Spates :

Question. Did you or not attend at the polls in said Election District, in Allegany county, on the 6th day of November 1866, if so, did you then and there offer a ticket to the Judges of Election at said polls, as your ballot, and was it received or rejected ; state also, the name of the person printed on said ticket for State Senate, for whom you desired to vote, and what reason did the judges assign for rejecting your vote, if they did so reject it?

Answer. I did attend at the polls on the 6th of November, 1866, in my District, and I offered my ticket to the Judges of Election, at the polls and they would not receive it. The name of the person printed on my ticket so offered as State Senator, was Alfred Spates. I offered my ticket to Mr. Friend, one of the judges, and he looked at me, and then looked at Mr. Kitzmiller, one of the other judges, and asked him if I was not on that list. Mr. Kitzmiller said that I was, and that he would not receive my ticket.

Cross-examined by Dr. Ohr.

By Dr. Ohr:

Question. Do you or not know whether your name was entered on the registration book of 1865, and what entry was made opposite to it?

Answer. I do not know, and have no knowledge of it.

By Dr. Ohr:

Question. Did the said judges require you to take an oath or do any other thing, before they rejected your vote?

Answer. They did not.

H. O. HAMILL.

Test:—J. J. McHENRY, Clerk.

December 6, 1866.

No other witnesses being produced by either parties, the examination is closed, at this place.

Given under my hand and seal this sixth day of December, in the year of our Lord, eighteen hundred and sixty-six.

J. M. STRONG, [SEAL.]

Oakland, Allegany county, Md., ✦

December 6, 1866.

[U. S. 5 ct. stamp.]

———

COURT HOUSE, CUMBERLAND,

ALLEGANY COUNTY, MARYLAND,

December 10, 1866.

In pursuance of the aforegoing notice, I attended also, at the time and place secondly therein designated, and having appointed said James J. McHenry, my clerk, and administered to him an oath to fairly write down and transcribe the depositions to be taken by me, did proceed then and there to take the following testimony, to wit:

Deposition No. 1.

HENRY D. CARLETON, having been by me duly sworn and examined, deposed and said as follows, to wit:

By Mr. Spates:

1st Question. What is your name, age, occupation and residence?

Answer. My name is Henry D. Carleton; age 58 years; occupation bailiff to the Corporation of Cumberland; residence in Cumberland, Maryland.

By Mr. Spates:

2d Question. Did you or did you not examine and count certain ballots and inspect the poll books therewith filed in the office of the Clerk of the Circuit Court for Allegany county on the 17th day of November, 1866; if so, state at whose instance you did so, who assisted you and what was the result of such count and inspection? State your knowledge fully and at large?

Answer. At the request of Colonel Spates, I went to the Clerk's office in Cumberland, and assisted in the inspection and count of tickets produced there and shown to me, on Saturday the 17th day of November, 1866. Charles F. Bean, produced to those assembled there, to wit: John H. Young, Thomas E. Gonder, Theodore A. Ogle, George W. Hoover, and A. M. Adams, the tickets and poll books of the sixteenth election District, in Allegany county, returned by the Judges of the election held November 6th, 1866; the tickets cast or voted in each election District, were counted seperately, commencing with election District No. 1; the part I performed was the inspecting each ticket as called off and counted, so as to see that the count was correct. I know that the names were called out correctly by the person who called out the names printed on the tickets so examined; the names printed on the ballots, were called out by A. M. Adams and Thomas E. Gonder. Theodore A. Ogle and George W. Hoover, acted as tellers in scoreing and keeping the tally or count.

The result as ascertained by the whole count, inspection and tally, was as follows:

Districts.	Col. Spates.	Dr· Ohr.
No. 1,	49	69
" 2,	62	.116
" 3,	127	155
" 4,	226	223
" 5,	307	390
" 6,	355	219
" 7,	83	52
" 8,	38	44
" 9,	114	103
" 10,	13	69

" 11,	95	68
" 12,	196	101
" 13,	452	372
" 14,	12	78
" 15,	77	96
" 16,	136	152
Total	2,342	2,307

Showing a majority in Col. Spates' favor of thirty-five (35) votes, over Dr. Ohr for State Senator.

Cross-examined by Dr. Ohr.

By Dr. Ohr:

Question. State in what this count differed from the returns made by the Judges?

Answer. In District No. 5, the count by the Judges was 296 votes for Spates, in the re-count made by myself and others, it was 307 votes for Spates; in the return made by the Judges, 399 votes were for Dr. Ohr; in the re count made by myself and others, it was 390 votes for Dr. Ohr. In District No. 6, the count made by the Judges was 352 votes for Spates, in the re-count made by myself and others, it was 355 votes for Spates; in the returns made by the Judges, 225 votes were for Dr. Ohr, in the re-count, it was 219 votes for Dr. Ohr. In District No. 12, the return made by the Judges of votes for Col. Spates was correct; for Dr. Ohr, it was 102 votes made by the Judges, the re-count made it 101 votes for Dr. Ohr. In District No. 13, the return made by the Judges, was 449 votes for Spates, in the re-count, we made it 452 votes for Spates; the Judges returned in this District, 383 votes for Dr. Ohr, and the re-count made it 372 votes for Dr. Ohr. All the other Districts were correctly counted by the Judges.

H. D. CARLETON.

Deposition No. 2.

JOHN H. YOUNG, having been by me duly sworn, deposed and said as follows, to wit:

By Mr. Spates:

Question. What is your name, age, occupation and residence?

Answer. My name is John H. Young; age 51 years, occupation, Postmaster at Cumberland, where I reside.

By Mr. Spates:

Question. Did you or did you not examine and count certain ballots and inspect the poll books filed therewith in the office of the Clerk of the Circuit Court for Allegany county, on the 17th day of November, 1866; if yea, state at whose instance you did so; who assisted you and what was the result of such count and inspection; state your knowledge fully?

Answer. On the 17th day of November, 1866, at the request of Col. A. Spates, I was invited to the Clerk's office of Allegany county, for the purpose of assisting to count and inspect the ballots from the 16 election Districts of Allegany county, to ascertain the number of votes given for Dr. Ohr and Alfred Spates, for the Senate of Maryland; when I came to the office, I found Messrs. Gonder, Adams, Ogle, Hoover, Carleton, Col. Spates and also Mr. Bevans and Mr. Bean, deputy Clerks in the Clerk's office.

The ballots and poll books were handed to us, severally, when we commenced to count the ballots, Messrs. Gonder and Adams calling the names, myself looking on to see that the name given was correct on the ballot, Mr. Hoover and Mr. Ogle were the tellers. After the whole number of tickets were counted, and the tellers agreeing in their count, the result was as follows, namely : 2,342 votes for Spates, and 2,307 votes for Dr. Ohr, precisely as testified to by Henry D. Carleton, just examined.

Cross-examination by Dr. Ohr waived.

JOHN H. YOUNG.

Deposition No. 3.

A. M, ADAMS, having been by me duly sworn, deposed and said as follows, to wit:

1st Question by Mr. Spates :

Question. What is your name, age, occupation and residence ?

Answer. My name is A. M. Adams, aged 50 years, occupation teacher, and residence Cumberland, Maryland.

2nd Question by Mr. Spates :

Did you or did you not examine and count certain ballots and inspect the poll books filed therewith in the office of the Clerk of the Circuit Court for Allegany county, on the 17th day of November, 1866 ? if so, state at whose instance you did so, who assisted you, and what was the result of such count and inspection ? State your knowledge, fully.

Answer. I was requested by Col. Spates to come over and assist in counting the tickets ; Messrs. Ogle and Hoover acted as tellers ; Mr. Young and Mr. Carleton acted as inspectors ; the ballots shown us were counted and tallied, in the Clerk's office, in our presence ; and, to the best of my recollection now, having taken no note of it, Col. Spates had a majority of the votes so counted, of thirty-five or thirty-seven votes for State Senator ; I have just heard the testimony of John

H. Young, just examined, and concur in his statement given here.

Cross-examination waived by Dr. Ohr.

` A. M. ADAMS.

Deposition No. 4.

THOMAS E. GONDER, having been by me duly sworn, deposed and said as follows, to wit :

1st Question by Mr. Spates :

What is your name, age, occupation and residence?

Answer. My name is Thomas E. Gonder, age 23 years, occupation, clerk of the Corporation of Cumberland, and law student, residence Cumberland, Md.

2d Question by Mr. Spates :

(Same as to other witnesses.)

Answer. On the 17th of November, 1866, at the request of Col. Spates, I came to the Clerk's office of Allegany county for the purpose of recounting the votes cast in the Election Districts of Allegany county, in the late election ; and counted the votes as cast by districts, being assisted by Mr. A. M. Adams. We began with District No. 1, counting all the districts, ending with the 16th ; Mr. Adams counted the majority of the districts ; Mr. Hoover and Mr. Ogle acted as tellers ; Mr. Carleton and Mr. Young looking on as inspectors. In four districts, the first four, our count corresponded exactly with the count returned by the Judges of Election for those four districts ; in district No. 5 there was a difference in the count made by us and by the Judges of Election ; in order to satisfy ourselves, we counted the district over twice, and the result was as follows : The count on the tally book of the Judges of Election was 399 for Dr. Ohr, and the count made by us showed a return of only 390 for Dr. Ohr : the count on the tally book for Col. Spates was 296—the count made by us was 307 : the certificate returned by the Judges of Election in this district made no mention of the vote for State Senate, at all ; all the other districts, except No. 13, I swear to the result of or confirm the statement with regard to them made by the other witnesses, Carleton, Young and Adams ; I have some doubt about No. 13—there may be a vote more or less—either for Dr. Ohr or for Col. Spates ; I think there was a mistake in our count, of one or perhaps two votes in this district.

THOS. E. GONDER.

Deposition No. 5.

THEODORE A. OGLE, a witness of lawful age, having been by me duly sworn, deposed and said as follows, to wit ;

By Mr. Spates :

Question. What is your name, age, occupation and residence?

Answer. My name is Theodore A. Ogle; age 40 years; occupation saddle and harness maker; residence, Cumberland, Maryland.

By Mr. Spates :

Question. Did you or did you not examine and count certain ballots and inspect the poll books filed therewith in the office of the Clerk of the Circuit Court for Allegany County, on the 17th day of November, 1866; if yea, state at whose instance you did so, who assisted you and what was the result of such count and inspection; state your knowledge fully?

Answer. On the 16th day of November, 1866, I was invited by Colonel A. Spates to come to the Clerk's Office of Allegany county, on the 17th of the same month, to assist in recounting and inspecting the ballots of the sixteen Election Districts of said county, to ascertain the number of votes given for Dr. C. H. Ohr and Colonel A. Spates, respectively, for State Senator, at the recent election in Maryland; I came to the office on said day as requested, and assisted Messrs. H. D. Carleton, A. M. Adams, J. H. Young, T. E. Gonder and George W. Hoover, the latter of whom acted as a teller with myself. The ballots were counted by the above named parties in the presence of Messrs. Bean and Bevans, Deputy Clerks, with the result as already given by the other witnesses examined here to-day. I kept one of the tallies now here exhibited, with my name endorsed thereon, in my own handwriting, and I now file with the Justice of the Peace the tally so kept by me as aforesaid.

Cross-examination by Dr. Ohr Waived.

THEO. A. OGLE.

Deposition No. 6.

GEORGE W. HOOVER, having been by me duly sworn, deposed and said as follows, to wit :

By Mr. Spates :

Question. What is your name, age, occupation and residence?

Answer. My name is George W. Hoover; age 38 years; occupation, Register of Wills for Allegany county; residence Cumberland, Maryland.

By Mr. Spates :

Question. Did you or did you not examine and count certain ballots and inspect the poll books filed therewith in the office of the Clerk of the Circuit Court for Allegany county, on the 17th day of November, 1866 ; if yea, state at whose

instance you did so, who assisted you and what was the result of such count and inspection; state your knowledge fully ?

Answer. My testimony and answer to this interrogatory is
about the same as that of Theodore A. Ogle, just examined.
At the request of Col. Spates I went to the Clerk's Office on
the 17th of November, 1866, and assisted in a recount of the
votes cast in Allegany county, at the election held therein on
the 6th of November, 1866. We counted the votes given respectively for Dr. Ohr and Col. Spates, for State Senator. Messrs.
Carleton, Adams, Young, Gonder and Ogle, witnesses already examined here, assisted in the count. I was one of the
tellers and Mr. Ogle was the other. The ballots were carefully counted and scrutinized, and the result, after a strict
count and examination, was, as detailed by the other witness, a majority of 35 votes for State Senator for Col. Alfred
Spates over Dr. Ohr. During the count and inspection of
the votes aforesaid, either Mr. Bean or Mr. Bevans, Deputy
Clerks, were present in the room with us and saw us making
the count and examining the votes. I kept a tally list, which
I here file with the Justice of the Peace, endorsed with my
name, in my own handwriting.

Cross-examination waived by Dr. Ohr.

GEO. W. HOOVER.

Deposition No. 7.

CHARLES F. BEAN, having been by me duly sworn, deposed
and said as follows, to wit :
By Mr. Spates :
Question. What is your name, age, occupation and resi-
dence ?
Answer. My name is Charles F. Bean; age 20 years; occupation, Deputy Clerk in the office of the Clerk of the Circuit
Court for Allegany county, Maryland, and I reside in Cumberland.
By Mr. Spates :
Question. Did or did not the Return Judges of the election
held on the 6th of November, 1866, in Allegany county,
Maryland, file with the Clerk of said county any ballots and
poll books; if so, who received them, where were they placed;
under whose control have they remained ever since ?
Answer. The said Judges of Election did deposit votes and
poll books with said Clerk, on the 10th day of November,
1866 I received a part of them from said Judges, and
Henry Bevans, another Deputy Clerk in the office with me,
received the balance, and all were deposited by me in the
ballot box kept in the vault attached to the Clerk's Office,
where they have remained ever since, locked up, except as

9

hereinafter stated. The key of the said ballot box is kept in the Clerk's Office.

By Mr. Spates:

Question. Did you or not, on the 17th November, 1866, attend at the examination and inspection of the votes and poll books; conducted by Messrs. Cárleton, Young, Adams, Ogle, Gonder and Hoover, on that day; if so, what ballots and poll books, if any, did you deliver to them to be counted and inspected?

Answer. I did attend at that inspection on that day. I was not there the whole time, but when I went out from there I left Henry Bevans, another Deputy Clerk, in my place until I returned. I saw the above named parties counting the votes and inspecting the poll books they had before them at that time. It was I who saw these ballots and poll books taken out of the ballot box, and they are the same that were returned by the Judges of Election, as stated in my answer to the third question above. I delivered the said ballot box to them, the parties above named, and saw them take the ballots and poll books out of it and count them. After these parties had counted the ballots, the ballots and poll books were returned to and deposited in the ballot box aforesaid, and are now in the Clerk's Office, locked up. Subsequent to the said examination, John Fay, a Deputy Clerk in the office with me, took the ballots out of the ballot box and afterwards replaced them in it, for the purpose of making a copy of some of the papers therein. I am a Deputy Clerk in the Clerk's Office of Allegany county.

Cross-examined by Dr. Ohr

By Dr. Ohr.

Question. Did any person or persons, between the 10th and 17th day of November, 1866, after the poll books and ballots had been deposited with you, examine the said poll books and ballots, deposited by the return judges of election, held in Allegany county, Maryland, November 6th, 1866; if so, name him or them, and when it was done and who was present?

Answer. No, not to my knowledge.

By Dr. Ohr.

Question. Have you or any of the other deputy Clerks, now in the said Clerk's office, of the Circuit Court for Allegany county, named in the foregoing depositions, been sworn as such?

Answer. I have not been sworn as such. I don't know whether or not the others have been sworn as such deputy Clerks or not.

By Dr. Ohr.

Question. If they had been would you not likely know it?

Answer. I know now that Mr. Bevans and Mr. Fay, above spoken of are sworn deputies. I did not know it when I answered the former question.

By Dr. Ohr.

Question. Who is the chief deputy Clerk in said Clerk's office?

Answer. There is no chief deputy—all act alike.

CHAS. T. BEAN.

Test—J. J, McHENRY, Clerk.

December, 29th, 1866.

[U. S. 5 ct. Stamp.]

Alfred Spates here files with me, J. M. Strong, Justice as aforesaid, certain papers, to be used as evidence in this case, same being marked "Exhibits Nos. 3, 4, 5, 6, 7, 8, 9, 10 and 11," and endorsed by me as filed with me by said Spates, at the date thereon endorsed.

There being no other witnesses to be examined, and said Alfred Spates not desiring further time for the production of evidence, I closed the said taking of testimony, and return the depositions so taken by me, closed up under my hand and seal, this 29th day of December, A. D. 1866.

And I also return herewith the poll books used, and the ballots cast at the late election in Allegany county, on the 6th day of November, 1866, as the same were delivered to me by Horace Resley, Clerk of the Circuit Court for Allegany county, aforesaid.

J. M. STRONG, [SEAL.]
Justice of the Peace, of the State of
Maryland, in and for Allegany county.

STATE OF MARYLAND,
Allegany County, to wit:

I hereby certify that Jos. M. Strong, Esq., before whom the annexed affidavits were made, and who has thereto subscribed his name, was at the time of so doing, a Justice of the Peace, of the State of Maryland, in and for Allegany county, duly commissioned and sworn.

In testimony whereof, I hereto set my hand [SEAL] and affix the seal of the Cirucit Court for Allegany county, this 29th day of December, 1866.

HORACE RESLEY, Clerk.

[U. S. 5 ct. Stamp.]

TO THE PRESIDENT
OF THE SENATE OF MARYLAND.

STATE OF MARYLAND,
Allegany County, to wit :

I, Joseph M. Strong, a Justice of the Peace of the State of Maryland, in and for Allegany county, duly commissioned and sworn, do hereby certify, that after application made to me by Charles H. Ghr, claimant of the office of Senator for Allegany county, I caused to be served on Alfred Spates, contestant of the election of said Ohr, as such Senator, notification, (a copy of which with the admission of service by said Alfred Spates, endorsed thereon, marked "Claimant's Exhibit A," hereunto annexed,) requiring him to attend at the Court House in Cumberland, in said county, on the day and at the place specified in said notification, to cross-examine the witnesses therein named.

I further certify, that the witnesses whose depositions are herewith returned, begining on page 1, and continuing by consecutive pages to page 53, were first by me duly sworn to testify truly and fully in the matter of the contest referred to in the notification hereto attached; that I caused the testimony of the said witnesses together with the questions propounded by the parties, or their attorney, to be reduced to writing in my presence, and in the presence of the parties or their attorneys, by the witnesses themselves, or by John Gephart, who was first sworn, fairly to write down and transcribe the deposition of witnesses; that the deposition of each witness was taken down in pursuance thereof, and at the time and place mentioned in the notification aforesaid, that each witness signed his deposition in my presence, after the same had been read to him.

I further certify, the papers marked "Claimant's Exhibit A," was filed by the claimant on the date marked thereon.

In testimony whereof, I here unto subscribe my name and seal at Cumberland, this —— day of December, in the year of our Lord, eighteen hundred and sixty-six.

J. M. STRONG,   [SEAL.]
A Justice of the Peace for the State of Maryland,
in and for Allegany county.

STATE OF MARYLAND,

ALLEGANY COUNTY, *to wit:*

ALFRED SPATES, ⎫
           ⎪ Contested Election for Senator from
   vs.   ⎬
           ⎪ Allegany county.
CHARLES H. OHR. ⎭

SIR: You are hereby notified in accordance with the provisions of Sections 57 and 59, of Article 35, of the Code of Public General Laws of Maryland, that an examination of the following witnesses, to wit: George W. McCulloh, James L. Hoblitzell, Caleb Dorety, Michael Sherry, Wm. Conrad, Wharton Mason, Douglas Perry, Neil J. Berston, Wm. Devecman, Joseph A. Cahill, C. M. Thruston, John H. Young, Chas. F. Bean, A. M. Adams, Theodore A. Ogle, Henry R. Atkinson, Daniel C. Bruce, Henry Bevans, John Boward, John Fay, Jos. M. Koerner, A. J. Clarke, L. W. Brant, Thos. Reid, Will H. Lowdermith and William Staples, will take place at the Court house in the city of Cumberland, Allegany county, Maryland, on Wednesday, the 26th day of December, 1866, at 10 o'clock, A. M.; by these witnesses, Charles H, Ohr, expects to prove that the third alledged ground set forth in your notice of contest, is not true and did not occur, and that you were not, and constitutionally and legally, could not be elected as Senator for said Allegany county.

And you are further notified as aforesaid, that on Thursday, the 27th day of December, 1866, at 10 o'clock, A. M., at the same place above mentioned, the following witnesses will be examined, to wit: James W. Furlon, Griffin Twigg, Lloyd Stallings, James M. Mathews, John H. Stallings, Capt. J. Morrow and James Mathews, of District No. 7, in said county, by these witnesses, Charles H. Ohr, expects to prove that by threats, violence and deportment of a large number of men of Conservative politics, legal voters,who would have voted for Charles H. Ohr for State Senator, were prevented from offering or tendering their ballots to the judges of election at the polls in said Election District No. 7, and that by the threats, violence and deportment above mentioned, a large number of illegal ballots were cast at said polls for Alfred Spates, for State Senator, at the election held on the sixth day of November, 1866.

If all the witnesses cannot be examined on the days named, then the examination to be continued from day to day, until the examination shall be completed.

You are required to attend at the above mentioned times and place, either in person or by attorney, to cross-examine witnesses.

Given under my hand and seal, this 15th day of December, 1866.

J. M. STRONG.   [Seal.]

A Justice of the Peace of the State of Maryland,
in and for Allegany county.

I hereby certify, that I served a notice similar to the within, upon Alfred Spates, at Cumberland, Allegany county, Maryland, on the 15th day of December, 1866.

DAVID STRONG, Constable.

Sworn to before me this 28th day of December, in the year of our Lord, eighteen hundred and sixty-six.

J. M. STRONG.   [Seal.]

Justice of the Peace of the State of Maryland,
in and for Allegany county.

Interrogatories to be propounded in case of Alfred Spates vs. C. H. Ohr, Contested Election.

SCHEDULE A.

CUMBERLAND, MD., December 26, 1866.

Interrogatory 1. What is your name, age, occupation residence, and time of such residence?

Interrogatory 2. Was you appointed an officer of registration for said Election District, did you qualify as such and discharge the duties of said officer of registration for and in said District; if so, state the year for which you so acted and whether you had read the Constitution and law regulating the registration of voters before entering on the discharge of the duties of said office, and did you administer the oath of voters as prescribed in Article 1, section 4, of the Constitution of Maryland, to each person before entering his name in the eighth column of the book of registration, or on the list of qualified voters, and did you give notice as required by law of the times and places of registration?

Interrogatory 3. Did you or did you not enter in the eighth column of the book of registration, or on the list of qualified voters for said District, the names of persons whose names had previously been entered or registered as disloyal; if so, state your authority and reason for so doing, fully and in detail, with the names of the persons so entered?

Interrogatory 4. Did you enter on your said book of registration, any names not before entered, and register them as qualified voters; if so, were they persons who were of lawful age and had legal residence in said District, before the 1st day of November, 1865; if so, name them and give your reasons and authority for so doing?

Interrogatory 5. Was you registered as a voter before the first day of August, 1866, and did you vote for State Senator at the election on the 6th day of November, 1866; if so, for whom did you so vote?

Interrogatories to be Propounded.

SCHEDULE B.

Interrogatory 1. What is your name, age, occupation, residence and time of such residence?

Interrogatory 2. Was you a Judge of Election for said Election District on the 6th day of November, 1866; if so, did the judges of the said election make public a declaration that all persons who had been registered in 1866 would, by them, be required to take the oath of voters, as prescribed in Article 1, section 4, of the Constitution of Maryland; if so, for what reason; and did the said Judges of election have armed men placed at the doors or windows of the place where the polls were held, or authorize them to be so placed; if so, state the reasons?

Interrogatory 3. Did you as a judge of said election refuse or reject the ballot tendered by any person whose name appeared on the list of qualified voters unconditionally and peremptorily and without requiring them to take any oath; if so, whom and for what reasons?

Interrogatory 4. Did you see or hear of any violence, intimidation or threats used by any person or persons to deter or intimidate persons from offering their votes; if so, state the name or names of the persons so prevented, and by whom used, and was the election on the 6th of November, 1866, as quiet and orderly as usual at your said polls?

Interrogatory 5. Is it or not, customary for the people of your District to carry their guns with them to public gatherings more particularly at that season of the year, and was there an unusual display of guns on the day of election, was there any special reason therefor; if so, state the reason fully and whether the armed men were of one or both political parties and give their names?

Interrogatory 6. Did you hear any discharge of fire arms on the day of said election near the polls; if so, under what citcumstances, in what manner, and by whom?

Interrogatories to be Propounded for District No. 10.

SCHEDULE C.

Interrogatory 1. What is you name, age, occupation, residence, and time of such residence?

Interrogatory 2. Did you attend the polls of said District on the 6th day of November, 1866, was you a legally registered voter, did you vote on said day for State Senator and for whom.

Interrogatory 3. How long did you remain at the said polls, did you see any person prevented from offering to vote by threats, violence or intimidation of any other person or persons; if so, state whom and by whom, and was or was not the election conducted as quietly and orderly as usual, at the said polls?

Interrogatory 4. Is it, or is it not customary for the people of your District to carry their guns with them to public gatherings more particularly at that season of the year, and was there an unusual display of guns about the polls, was there any special reason therefor; if so, state the reasons fully?

Interrogatory 5. How far do you reside from the place where the polls were held, was it the usual place of holding said polls, and the place advertised by the Sheriff for that purpose, and how far is it from the Virginia line.

Interrogatories to be Propounded.

SCHEDULE D.

Interrogatory 1tt. What is your name, age, occupation, residence and time of such residence?

Interrogatory 2d. Was you appointed Judge of Election for said Election District of Allegany county, in 1866; did you qualify and act as such judge at the election held on the 6th day of November, and after closing the polls did you then and there carefully and correctly read, tally and count the ballots cast at said election, and write down the true number of votes cast for Alfred Spates and Charles H. Ohr, respectively, for State Senator, and did you return the said and identical ballots to the office of the Clerk of the Circuit Court for Allegany county; state fully your mode of counting and preserving said ballots, who were present and exercising a supervision over said reading and tally?

Interrogatory 3rd. Who acted as clerks at said election, and to what political party do they belong?

Interrogatory 4th. Did you attend the polls for said Election District No. 5, in Allegany county, Maryland, on the 6th day of November, 1866, and did you see the ballots cast at said election, read, tallied and counted, were they carefully and correctly read by the judges, and tallied and counted by the Clerks of Election on that occasion; state fully their mode of proceeding; to what political party do you belong; and for whom did you vote for State Senator?

Interrogatory 5th. Did the number of ballots in the ballot box of said district at the close of the polls, and count, agree with the number of persons who voted ; if not, state the difference fully ; if there were any deceitfully folded tickets, what did you do with them, and whose name was on them for State Senator?

———————

Interrogatories to be propounded for C. H. Ohr vs. Alfred Spates.

SCHEDULE E.

Interrogatory 1st. What is your name, age, occupation, residence and time of such residence?

Interrogatory 2nd. Are you, or was you acting as deputy clerk in the office of the Clerk of the Circuit Court for Allegany county, when did you enter on service in said office, and when were you sworn as such?

Interrogatory 3rd. Did you receive from the Judges of election the poll books and ballots of the election held on the 6th day of November 1866; when did you receive them, and what disposition did you make of them, who examined them after they were received and prior to the 17th day of November 1866, and in whose presence?

Interrogatory 4th. Did you after the election on the 6th day of November 1866, at any time see the poll books and ballots of said election or either of them; if so, at what times and under what circumstances; state fully where you saw them, in what condition; and who, if any one, had them in hand and who was present?

10

TESTIMONY.

———

Depositions taken on behalf of C. H. Ohr in contested election of Alfred Spates vs. said Ohr, for State Senator for Allegany coun'y, at Cumberland, on the 26th, 27th, 28th and 29th of December 1866.

R. W. MASON,

1st Interrog. What is your name, age, occupation, residence and time of such residence?

, Answer. Robt. Wharton Mason, age 43 years, clerk, Frostburg Election District No. 5, resided therein fifteen years.

2nd Interrog. Was you appointed an officer of said District.

Interrogatory 2nd, as in scedule A, excepted by Alfred Spates?

Answer. I was so appointed. I did act as register in 1865; I had read the Constitution and Law; relating to registration; it was administered by me or one of the other officers of registration to each person. But was absent on the 1st day of registration, being sick; I did give notice as required by law.

3rd Interrog. Was you appointed clerk at the election, held in said District the 6th day of November 1866; did you qualify and act as such?

Answer. Interrogatory 3rd excepted to by A. Spates.

Answer. I was, and did.

4th Interrog. As No. 5, in Schedule D.

Answer. I did attend the polls, I heard them read, I saw them tallied and counted, but of course could not see what was on the tickets; I heard every ticket read, and they were carefully tallied and counted by the clerks, one of the Judges, stood by the box and took out the tickets and opened them, and handed them to the 2nd, who read them, read each name and ticket seperately, but whether they read them correctly or not I cannot say, and the 3rd one strung them; I belong to the Union or Republican party, and voted for C. H. Ohr, for State Senator.

Cross-examined by Col. A Spates.

1st Interrog. Did you receive a commission from the Governor of Maryland, to act as register in Allegany county, if so, did you take an oath for the faithful performance of said duty before the clerk of the Circuit Court of Allegany county ?

Answer. I received a commission from the Governor commissioning me as register, but did not take any oath for the faithful performance of said duty before the clerk of the Circuit Court of Allegany county, but before a Justice of the Peace.

R. W. MASON.

Deposition No. 2.

HENRY R. ATKINSON, (Sworn.)

Interrogatory 1st. To Interrogatory 1st, as in schedule A, he answers and says, Henry Richard Atkinson, age 46 years, occupation clerk, residence, Election District No. 5, in Allegany county, Maryland, I have resided 5 years, in that District?

Interrogatory 2nd. To Interrogatory 2nd, as in schedule A, he answers and say;

(Excepted to by Mr. A. Spates.)

I was, I did in 1866, I had, I did, I did.

Interrogatory 3rd. To Interrogatory 3rd, as in schedule A, he answers and says;

(Excepted to by Mr. A. Spates.)

I did enter some in the eighth column that had been rejected by the registers the year before, my reason for so doing was because there was not sufficient evidence before me in my judgement to disqualify them, about ten in number, all of which will appear by the book of registration, returned to the clerk of the Circuit Court of Allegany county.

Interrogatory 4th. To Interrogatory 4, as in schedule A, he answers and says;

(Excepted to by A. Spates.)

I did enter the names of some who had not been registered before.

Interrogatory 5th. To Interrogatory 5th, as in schedule A, he answers and says: I was registered before the 1st day of August 1866, and I did vote for Alfred Spates for State Senator?

Cross-questioned by A. Spates.

I did receive a commission from the Governor to act as register in Allegany county, and I qualified before the clerk of the Circuit Court of Allegany county, on the 27th day of July 1866, within 30 days from the date of the commission, and here produce the record of qualification.

HENRY R. ATKINSON.

Wm. Conrad, (sworn) :
Interrogatory 1st, as in Schedule D, he answers and says :
Wm. Conrad, my age 69 years, my occupation contractor,
my residence Frostburg, Election District No. 5, Allegany
county, Md., and have lived there five years or more.
Interrogatory 2nd, as in Schedule D, he answer and says :
I was appointed Judge of Election District No. 5 and did
qualify and act as such Judge ; after closing the polls I did
read between three and four hundred of said ballots, and requested Mr. Hoblitzell to look over my shoulder ; I saw the
votes carefully tallied and counted ; I saw the clerks write
down the true number of votes cast for Alfred Spates and C.
H. Ohr, respectively, for State Senator ; I did return the said
identical ballots to the Clerk of the Circuit Court for Allegany county ; Mr. Benjamin Thomas took them out of the
box, and I read them slow, and then handed them to William Staples, the other Judge, to be strung. Mr. J. J. Hoblitzell, G. W. McCulloh, C. Douty, D. C. Bruce and M.
Sherry were present at their reading.
Interrogatory 3d, as in Schedule D, he answers and says :
The ballots did agree with the names of the voters.

Cross-questioned by A. Spates.

To the first cross-interrogatory to William Conrad on the
part of A. Spates, he answers and says : I did act as Return
Judge for that district, and I and my fellow Judges did make
a true return of the number of votes cast for each party voted
for, respectively ; we signed the return, and I returned it to
the Clerk's office as Return Judge.
To the second interrogatory to William Conrad on the
part of A. Spates, he answers and says : Returns shown to
the Judge of Election District No. 5, who admits that it is
his handwriting to the returns, but that the Senators were
omitted from the certificate ; A. Spates files a certified copy
of said return, as shown to the witness.

Re-examination of William Conrad.

Interrogatory 4th of Schedule D :
(Excepted to by A. Spates.)
R. W. Mason and John C. Wise, who acted as clerks at
said election, Mason a Radical and Wise a Democrat.
WILLIAM CONRAD.

Re-examination of R. W. Mason.

Interrogatory 1st. How did it happen that you omitted
the vote for Senator, in your certificate or return of votes
polled at the election in District No. 5, held on the 6th of
November, 1866 ?

(Excepted to by A. Spates.)

Answer. John C. Wise, the other clerk, drew up the certificate attached to his poll book, and I intended to copy the certificate from the Code ; he handed me the certificate he had written, from which I copied ; he signified 'twould be handier than to copy from the book.

Cross-examination of R. W. Mason by A. Spates.

Question. At what time did you finish counting the tickets, and who had charge of the tickets and ballot box from the time you closed counting until you saw Mr. Wise making out said returns referred to ; and were any of the Judges of Election present at the time when Mr. Wise wrote said certificate referred to by you ?

Answer. Closed, I think, about ten o'clock P. M. Wm. Conrad took charge of the ballots and the ballot box, but don't know what he did witn them ; did not make out the certificate of returns that night . I don't think any Judges of Election were present when Mr. Wise was making out this certificate of Returns as referred to ; do not think that there were any of the Judges of Election present when I made out my certificate, and I did not see any of the Judges sign the certificate of return ; the certificates were made out the morning after the election.

R. W. MASON.

CALEB DOUTY, (sworn) :
Interrogatory 1st, as No. 1, in Schedule D. Caleb Douty, age 47, occupation merchant, residence Frostburg, Allegany county, Md, and resided there nine months.
Interrogatory 2nd, as No. 5 in Schedule D. I was at the polls in the morning and voted ; I was in the room during the later part of the counting ; there was a great deal of care exercised during the counting and tallying of the ballots ; one of the Judges sat at the box, took out the ballots, opened them, and handed them to the second Judge, who read each name seperately, and was strung by the 3d Judge ; I am a Radical, and voted for Dr. C. H. Ohr.

Cross-examination of C. Douty by A. Spates.

Question. Did you or not keep a tally of the votes or ballots you saw counted out while present in said room ?

Answer. I did not.

C. DOUTY.

J. J. HOBLITZELL, (Sworn.)
Interrogatory 1st. As No. 1, in Schedule D. Jas. Jacob Hoblitzell, age 35, residence Frostburg, Allegany county, Maryland, occupation saddler, have resided there ᵃ years.

Interrogatory 2nd. As No. 5, in Schedule D. Did attend the polls on said day, I saw the ballots read, tallied and counted, they were carefully and correctly read by the judges, they were correctly tallied and counted by the clerks, to the best of my knowledge and belief, and do not think it could have been done more correctly, was looking over the reading and tallying at the request of one of judges, one of the judges took the ticket from the box and opened it and passed it to the other judge, who read the ticket carefully, and then passed it to the 3d judge, who strung it, some of the tickets were strung by M. Sherry, at the request of the judge; I am a Radical, and voted for Dr. C. H. Ohr.

Cross-examination of J. J. Hoblitzell by A. Spates.

Interrogatory 1st. Did you or not keep a tally of the ballots as counted out by the Judges of Election?

Answer. I did not keep a tally.

Interrogatory 2d. Were the tickets counted out that night, and state, if you know, what was done with them, and was Michael Sherry one of the Judges of Election?

Answer. The tickets were counted out that night, but I do not know what was done with them; Mr. Sherry was not one of the Judges of Election, but I saw him stringing the tickets during a portion of the time.

J. J. HOBLITZELL.

MICHAEL SHERRY, (Sworn.)

Interrogatory 1st. As No. 1, in Schedule D. My age, 53; occupation, Justice of the Peace, residence Frostburg, Allegany county, Maryland, and have resided there 30 years.

Interrogatory 2d. As in Schedule D. He answers and says:

Answer. I did attend the election on said day I saw the ballots read, tallied and counted, as far as I could see, they used a great deal of care in counting and tallying, the names were separately read, tallied and counted, one judge took the ballot from the box and opened it, and passed it to the second, who read it, and then passed it to the third, who strung the same, except for a portion of the time when, at the request of one of the judges; I strung a portion of the tickets, I belong to the Radical party, and voted for Dr. C. H. Ohr, for State Senator; and I think that they were correctly read and tallied.

Mr. Sherry cross-examined by A. Spates.

Interrogatory 1st. Did you not keep a tally of the tickets you saw counted; what was done with the tickets after they were counted, were they left in your office, and who had charge of them, while in your office, and who had the key of the office, and how many tickets did you string, and were you sworn?

Answer. I did not keep a tally; Mr. Conrad took charge of the tickets, but I do not know what he did with them, I do not know if they were in my office or not; I had the key of my office; don't know how many tickets I strung; I was not sworn. The polls were held in my office, was not a Judge of the Eelection.

M. SHERRY.

JOHN BOWARD, (Sworn.)

Interrogatory 1st. As in Schedule D. John Boward, my age, 64; occupation, cabinet maker; reside in District No. 6, of Allegany county, Maryland, have resided there upwards of 20 years.

Interrogtoary 2d. As in Schedule D:

Answer. I was appointed, qualified and acted as judge at said election. I took all the tickets out of the box, I opened them, and then handed them to Judge Reid, who read them all, he read each name separately, and then handed them to Judge Willison, who strung them, they were read correctly, and tallied correctly to the best of my knowledge, the count for Senator was correctly set down, I counted the tickets over after the election, and the vote for C. H. Ohr was correctly set down by the clerks; I did return the said and identical tickets to the Clerk of the Circuit Court for Allegany county.

To the 1st cross-interrogatory to J. Boward, answers and says: It was not possible for him to look over the ticket while the judge read it. It was not possible for me to see that the clerks put each persons vote down properly, I sat near enough to one clerk to have seen, but not near enough to the other, and I cannot say that I saw every vote put down properly.

Excepted to by C. H. Ohr.

To the 2d cross-interrogatory he answers and says: That he and his fellow judges did not count the tickets the second time, I was return judge, and with the assistance of two of the return judges, I made a re-count, when it appeared that there were two votes less for C. H. Ohr than had been certified to by the Judges of District No. 6; and in making this re-count the other judges several times stopped me, and informed me that I had turned two tickets at once, after this re-count, I took the tickets home, and counted them myself, and found them to agree with the 1st count as to the number of votes for C. H. Ohr, and it was so certified by the return judges. The tickets were counted three times, twice at the Court House, and once at my own house.

JOHN BOWARD.

THOMAS REID, Sworn :

Interrogatory 1st. As in Schedule D:

Answer. Thos. Reid ; my age, 55 years ; occupation, saddler; residence, District No. 6, in Allegany county; and have resided there 30 years.

Interrogatory 2d. As in Shedule D. He answers and says:

Answer. I was appointed, qualified and acted as such ; I read the tickets, each name carefully and correctly, and as far as I know they were properly tallied by the clerks.

(Excepted to by A. Spates.)

THOMAS REID.

JOSEPH M. KOERNER, (Sworn.)

Interrogatory 1st. As in schedule D.

James M. Koerner, age 38, occupation Wheelwright, residence District No. 13, of Allegany county, have resided there 9 years.

Interrogatory 2nd. As in schedule D.

(Excepted to by A. Spates.)

I was appointed, qualified and did act as Judge at said election, I carefully read the names on ballots, to the best of my knowledge they were carefully and correctly tallied, and counted, by the clerks; I was too far from the clerks to see that they were tallied correctly, I did return the tickets to the clerk of the Circuit Court for Allegany county, Maryland, A. J. Clark and Alfred Spates looked over A. J. Clarks shoulder for some time.

Interrogatory 3rd. As in schedule D. The number of ballots in the ballot box at the close of the polls, and count did not agree with the number of persons who voted, there were 843 names on the poll books, and on counting the tickets, we found 850 tickets in the ballot box, three of these tickets were double, which we threw away, and left 847, which we counted and strung, there was another deceitfully folded, as one of the Judges thought, but Mr. Clark thought it was not, and we counted it. It was a conservative ticket, and we counted both, the other three double tickets were also conservative tickets, the name of A. Spates was on them for State Senator.

To the 1st Cross-Interrogatory, he answers and says; we did not read each name on the tickets as written or printed respectively except the split tickets, but we put down the whole tickets without reading each name, but carefully examined them to see that they were whole tickets, as the tickets were drawn out, if it proved to be a split ticket it was put in a seperate box where the split tickets were kept, if it was a whole ticket, after being satisfied that it was a whole ticket, we put it down and the clerks tallied it without the names being read, except the heading of the same.

JOSEPH M. KOERNER.

Re-examination.

Interrogatory 1st. Were there any votes taken at the polls of District 13, which in your judgment were illegal; if so, state the number and the names of the persons so voting, and give your reasons fully for judging them illegal?

A. Spates excepts to the Interrogatory as embracing facts not embraced in the notice.

In my judgment there was one that I am fully satisfied had no right to vote in my District; the name of said party is Edward Williams, my reason is that he was a citizen of No. 6, and not of No. 13, and I protested against his vote; dont know to what political party he belonged, but he was in the Federal Army; I heard him talk but he did not talk as though he would vote the Union ticket.

To the 2nd Cross-Interrogatory on the part of Alfred Spates he says his name was on the list of registered voters for District No. 13; I belong to the Radical party, and voted for Dr. C. H. Ohr for State Senator.

JOSEPH M. KOERNER.

James M. Mathews, Sworn.

Interrogatory 1st. As No. 1, in schedule A. James M. Mathews, my age 49 years, occupation farmer, residence Election District No. 7, have resided there 49 years?

Interrogatory 2nd. As No. 2 in schedule A. A. Spates objects to that question, because there was no notice of the facts intended to be proved by that interrogatory contained in the notice to A. Spates given by Dr. C. H. Ohr, I was appointed and received a commission from the Governor to act as register for District No. 7, in Allegany county, Maryland, did qualify by taking the oath before a Magistrate, but did not qualify by taking the oath before the Clerk of the Circuit Court for Allegany county; I did discharge the duties as register in said district for the year of 1865. I had read the Constitution and Law regulating the registration of voters, we did administer the oath of voters, we did give notice as required by law of the time and place of registration.

Interrogatory 3rd. (Special,) Who acted as officer of registration in said District in 1866; was he registered in 1865, and how, A. Spates objects to this Interrogatory and its answer, because it is not embraced in the notice, and you cannot prove it by parole.

Answer. John Deffinburgh, and he was registered as disloyal 1865, under the 4th section of Article 1st, of the Constitution of Maryland, and said book of registration was produced.

Interrog. 4. As No. 2 in schedule D. (Excepted to by A. Spates as not in the notice.)

I was appointed Judge of said Election District in 1866.

11

I qualified and acted as such. We did, after closing the polls, carefully and correctly read, tally and count the ballots. Well, we did try to.

Interrog. 5. As No. 4 of schedule B. (Question objected to by A. Spates.)

Now, in the first place, it was a great trouble to get the Judges to organize at the election. Lloyd Stallings was Return Judge. He had the oath, all the papers and books, and it was getting late, and we organized; he being Return Judge, I expected him to do the business; he did not take any active part in the election at all. I was entirely on the inside of the house; I did not see or hear any violence, intimidation or threats used; the election on the 6th day of November, 18██, was as quiet as usual at our polls.

To the first cross interrogatory on the part of A. Spates to James M. Matthews, he answers and says: We took testimony, and took it in writing, in regard to his disloyalty; he did not apply for registration; he could not refuse to take the oath, because he was not there; Michael Twigg and Thomas Athey were the witnesses against him, but he was not present; I cannot produce the testimony as taken down, John H. Stallings took it down in pencil; I did not preserve it as taken down; I can't recollect what they testified against him; we sent no special notice to Diffinbaugh that his case was to come up on charges against him; we gave notice generally for the correction of errors and omissions.

JAMES M. MATHEWS.

LEVI W. BRANT, sworn.

Interrog. 1st. Schedule D.

Answer. Levi W. Brant; my age 45; occupation coal dealer; residence, Election District No. 13; have resided there ten or twelve years.

Interrog. 2d. Schedule D.

Answer. I was appointed Judge of Election for District No. 13, for 1866. I did qualify and act as such; to the best of my knowledge the ballots were carefully and correctly read, tallied and counted; I did not write them down, but I had an eye to the Clerks, and I think it was so done; but there is not a proper rotation of names on the poll books; I selected the full tickets from the box, passed them, after a careful examination, to Mr. Koerner, who read them aloud, giving the leading name on the ticket as being full; the split tickets, as I came to them, were deposited in a separate box until after the full tickets were counted out; the split tickets were then carefully examined by me and read by Mr. Koerner, in the presence of Mr. A. J. Clark, during the whole time, and Mr. Spates during a portion of the time.

Interrog. 3d. Schedule D.

The number of ballots in the box did not agree with the

number of persons who voted. The number of tickets deposited in the box was 853, and the voters · on the list was 843; there were three tickets folded double that were not counted; then I noticed in counting the tickets from the box one smaller folded inside of the other; when I unfolded this ticket I remarked to Mr. Clark that I thought it deceitfully folded together; but Mr. Clark thought not, so I passed them both to Mr. Koerner, who read them, and they were counted on the poll book. There were two other tickets of the same character that I noticed during the count, on which I made no remark; they were together in the same manner as the first; they were read and counted. Mr. Spates' name for Senator was on the first three which were thrown out and on the second three which were counted.

To the first cross interrogatory on the part of A. Spates, he answers and says: We did not read every name on every ticket singly; we separated them into whole and split tickets; putting the split tickets into a box used for the purpose; if it was a whole ticket we announced it whole Union or whole Democratic, and the Clerks registered accordingly.

Interrog. 2d. He answers and says: I do not think the Clerks omitted the names of any of the voters; it must have been done through the tickets.

·L. W. BRANT.

John H. Stallings, (Sworn) :

Interrogatory 1st. As in Schedule A.

Answer. John H. Stallings, age 44 years, occupation farmer, place of residence in Election District No. 7 in Allegany county, Maryland, have resided there fifteen years.

Interrogatory 2nd. As No. 2 in Schedule A.

(Interrogatory and answer objected to because the facts proposed to be elicited do not come within the notice given by Charles H. Ohr to A. Spates of the facts proposed to be proved by this witness.)

I was appointed an officer of Registration for said district; I did qualify as such before a Justice of the Peace, but did not qualify before the Clerk of the Circuit Court for Allegany county ; I received a commission from the Governor to act as such ; I acted for the year 1865 ; I had read the Constitution and Law regulating registration, repeatedly ; we did so administer the oath ; we gave notice as required by law as to the time and place of registration.

Interrogatory 3d (Special.) Who acted as officer of registration for said district in 1866 ; was he registered in 1865, and how ?

(Excepted to by A. Spates.)

Answer. I understood that John Diffenbaugh did act, but I know nothing about it, save from hearsay—book produced and identified—he was disfranchised for disloyalty by the testimony of Michael Twigg and Thomas W. Athey; he was not registered as a qualified voter.

To the first cross-interrogatory on the part of A. Spates he answers and says. We took the testimony in pencil writing; I think he did not apply for registration; he did not refuse to take the oath, for he was not present; the witnesses against him were Michael Twigg and Thomas W. Athey; Diffenbaugh was not present at the time; I can't tell what was taken down as testimony against him; I do not know where the testimony now is—I think it is in the hands of Squire Hartley; we did not summons any of the witnesses, nor did we give notice to Diffenbaugh that we were about to take up his case under charges; John Hartley was one of the registers with me.

JOHN H. STALLINGS.

GRIFFIN TWIGG, (Sworn):

Interrogatory 1st. As No. 1 in Schedule B. Griffin Twigg, age 47, occupation farmer, residence Election District No. 7 of Allegany county, Maryland, resided there over one year.

Interrogatory 2nd. As No. 2 in Schedule C. I did attend said polls on the 6th day of November, 1866; I was registered; I did not vote.

Interrogatory 3d. As No. 4 in Schedule B. John Carder, James Carder; they appeared to be the foremost at the polls; they ordered the Judges to take a vote, as they handed it in at the window; they made threats against any man saying anything against voters or challenging, and I understood these threats to be to the Judges; the vote offered was that of Samuel L. Wagner; do not know whether the Judges took the vote or not; Christopher Kelley talked pretty rough to me, and said if I interfered or challenged, and that no damn man dared come there to challenge at the polls that day; I had just challenged the vote of Samuel L. Wagner.

Interrogatory 4th, (Special.) Why did you not vote, and for whom would you have voted for State Senator?

Answer. I did not think that I was safe in going up to the polls and letting them surround me, and there was no other way in getting there, because I thought they would mob me if they could do it; I would have voted the full Union ticket; don't know to my own certain knowledge to what party they belong.

The 1st cross-interrogatory to Griffin Twigg by A. Spates: At what time did you return from Pennsylvania to Maryland: naming the day of the month; how long did you live in Pennsylvania; when were you registered, and by whom;

did you offer or tender your vote to the Judges of Election ;
how long were you at the polls on the day of election ; did
you see any person refused a vote on the day of election ; did
not Christopher Kelley advise you to go and vote ; state your
reason for refusing to vote ; did or did not Mr. Kelly state to
you that every man entitled to vote should vote ; and could
you not have voted if you offered ?

Answer. I cannot name the day nor day of the month, this
winter two years ago ; I lived in Pennsylvania about three
years ; moved there in 1861 ; I was registered in 1865 as a
non-resident, and 1866 as a voter, by John Diffenbaugh ; I
did not tender my vote ; I am not able to say how long I
was at the polls, not more than half an hour ; I suppose it
was in the morning ; I presume the polls had not long been
opened ; I did not see any person refused a vote on the day
of election ; I have no recollection of any such conversation
with Christopher Kelley ; I did not go to the polls after the
confusion and offer my vote ; I think he did not use that
language, hut that every damn man that was registered
should vote ; I think I could not have voted had I offered my
vote.

2d Cross-Interrogatory. What reason did you assign to the
Judges for challenging the vote of Samuel L: Wagner; was
he a citizen of the State and how long had he resided in the
county ?

Answer. I challenged his vote from the fact that I had understood that he was disfranchised the Fall before; I have
known him for about 30 years and as far as I know he has always resided in this county.

3d Cross-Interrogatory. At the time you challenged his
vote, did you known of your own knowledge anything or act
that he had committed, that ought to have deprived him of
his vote, if yea, state that act, or what those acts were, and
do you know now whether he was disfranchised or refused registration ?

Answer. I know of nothing particular; I do not know of
my own knowledge that he was refused registration.

4th Cross-Interrogatory. When you challenged his vote,
was or was not your object to create disturbance?

Answer. No, sir, it was not.

5th Cross-Interrogatory. In consequence of your challenging his vote, was a disturbance created that day, and if so,
what did you say and what did they say, and what was the
disturbance ?

Answer. I don't know that my challenging was the cause
of a disturbance that day ; I do not recollect of talking to
anybody at that time, but Christ. Kelly ; I was trying to reason the matter with him ; I suggested to him to listen to me,
but he would not listen to anything; Kelly said that any dam'd

man that was registered should vote; I do not recollect anything else that he said.

6th Cross-Interrogatory, Were you realy afraid to offer your vote, or was your fear feigned on purpose to create a disturbance?

Answer. I was realy afraid to offer my vote, for I believed that if I got into the polls where they could surround me that they would mob me.

7th Cross-Interrogatory. Are you naturally a man of nerve or a coward?

Answer. I am not fearful.

8th Cross-Interrogatory. Name the men that were at the polls that you were afraid of mobbing you?

Answer. Well there were a great many there, right smart crowd, Samuel L. Wagner, Christopher Kelly, James Wilson, Patrick Kelly, John Carder, James Carder, Simeon Twigg, and a number of others there that I did not know their faces.

9th Cross-Interrogatory. What did any one of those men say to you as a threat; who made the threat and what language was used in making it?

Answer. That Mr. Kelly said every dam'd man that was registered should vote, I do not know that any pointed threat was made toward me, I do not know that any of the others said anything to me particularly,.

GRIFFIN TWIGG.

JAMES W. FARLOW, sworn.

Interrogatory 1st. As in schedule B.

James W. Farlow; age 51; occupation farmer; and acting as constable in election District No. 7, of Allegany county, Maryland, have resided there about 7 years.

Interrogatory 2d. As No. 2, in schedule C.

I did attend the polls on the 6th of November, 1866; I was legally registered as far as I know; I voted the whole Union ticket.

Interrogatory 3d. As No. 4, in schedule B.

I did not; I was there but a very few minutes.

1st Cross-Interrogatory to James W. Farlow by A. Spates.

If it had not been for Griffin Twigg, would there have been in your opinion any excitement at the polls that day?

Answer. I do not know; I saw nothing of it.

JAMES W. FARLOW.

HENRY L. BEVANS, sworn.

Interrogatory 1st. As No. 1, in schedule E.

H. L. Bevans; age 22 years, occupation, Deputy Clerk of Allegany county, residence election District No. 6, in Allegany county, Maryland, have resided there 15 years.

Interrogatory 2d. As No. 2, in schedule E.

I am, and was acting as Deputy Clerk on the 15th of May, 1865, was sworn on the 10th day of December, 1866.

Interrogatory 3d. As No. 3, in schedule E.

I received a part of them; I received them on Saturday the 10th of November, 1866; I left them on the desk in the office and went to dinner, and Charley Bean said he would put them away; I don't know that any one examined them; but saw Mr. Spates and one of the Clerks with the poll books several times; the poll books and tickets were tied together, but I never saw him with the tickets, except the day they were counted, when I saw him in the vault; I do not remember whether he had the poll books; I saw Mr. Spates in the vault several times and once in company with J. P. Rowan; there is a Clerk always in the vault and when not there, it is locked up; the key of the vault is usually hung by the door in the office; any one acquainted about the office can get the key, and some times they go and take it, lawyers for instance: I never saw Mr. Spates take it.

Interrog. 4. As in Schedule E. I did; when they were first delivered there, and the day they counted the ballots of the whole county, they were counted by Mr. Young, G. Hoover. H. D. Carleton, A. M. Adams, T. A Ogle & Thos. E. Gindor.

Interrog. 5th. Was the Clerk of the Circuit Court; Mr. H. Resley; absent from the office, or from Cumberland, between the 10th and 17th days of November, 1866; if so, for how long

Answer. He was absent from the office, but do not remember whether from Cumberland or not; he was absent when they were counted; he was absent some parts of the days from the office; he generally came to the office in the morning, and then went over to the house he is building, sometimes he would stay at the office one hour, and sometimes nearly all day.

H. L. BEVANS.

JOHN B FAY, (Sworn.)

Interrog. 1st. In Schedule E. J. B. Fay; my age 23 years; my occupation, Deputy Clerk; residence in Election District No. 6, in Allegany county, Maryland, have resided here since August, 1866.

Interrog. 2. As in Schedule E. I am acting as such; entered the office on the 1st of October, 1866, I dont remember, but was sworn as such on the same day as Mr. Bevans was.

Interrog. 3. As in Schedule E. I received the poll books of District 1, and helped to file one or two others; I received them I think on Saturday the 10th, they were examined by a party in the vault on the 17th of November, I did not remain there, I simply went there on business; I cannot positively; I do not remember of any one handling them before that time, November 17.

Interrog. 4. As in Schedule E. I did see them on the day they were returned; I saw them afterward, for I made some copies of returns for Mr. Spates; I saw them at other times, I think I helped to make a search to see if one of the poll books was not missing; it was not missing, it was in the office.

Interrog. 5. as in deposition No. 15. He was absent from the office; he was gone nearly a week, perhaps a full week, which was between the 10th and 17th of November; I was absent myself on the 13th and 14th, and nearly all day on the 15th; my station is in the vault.

JNO B. FAY.

CHAS. F. BEAN, (Sworn.)

Interrog. 1st. as in Schedule E. Chas. F. Bean; age 20 years; occupation, deputy clerk; residence in Election District No. 6, in Allegany county, Md., have resided here about 2 years.

Interrog. 2. as in Schedule E. I am acting as such; entered in January, 1865; sworn as such on the 10th of December, 1866.

Interrog. 3d, as No 4, in Schedule E. I did see the poll books of the election on the 6th of November; I put them in the box, and took them out several times to make copies from the poll book; no one but the deputy clerks.

Interrog. 4th. as No. 5, in deposition No. 15. The clerk, Mr. H. Resley, was absent from Cumberland, between the 10th and 17th of November; he was absent four or five days, and perhaps longer. CHARLES F. BEAN.

WM. DEVECMON, (Sworn.)

Interrog. 1. as in Schedule D. Wm. Devecmon, age 23 years; occupation, lawyer; residence in Election District No. 6, in Allegany county Md.; have resided here all my life.

Interrog. 2, as No. 4, in Schedule D. I saw poll books in the clerk's office, but do not know whether they were of this election or not; they were on the back desk; saw some ballots; dont know which they were, saw them in the vault; John Fay was in the vault at the time; saw books and ballots together, when no one was in the vault.

WILLIAM DEVECMON.

A. M. ADAMS, (Sworn.)

Interrogatory 1st as No. 1, in schedule E. A. M. Adams, age 49 years, occupation School Teacher, residence in District No. 6, in Allegany county, Maryland, have resided there 33 years.

Interrogatory 2d, as No. 4, in schedule E. I was called upon by Mr. Spates to assist in recounting the ballots of the county. I saw the poll books and ballots, in the Vault, in the rear of the Clerk's office. The ballots were all in good condition except, probably, two or three ; they from some cause were probably detached. The ballots and poll books were not tied together. We counted the ballots to ascertain the number of votes, and compared it with the poll books.— At the time of the recount J. H. Young, T. A. Ogle, H. D. Carleton, George Hoover, Thomas E. Gonder and Mr. A. Spates, and the two deputy Clerks were present. The detached poll books and tickets of the two Districts agreed in the count ; the number of ballots agreed with the number of names on these poll books.

A. M. ADAMS.

Mr. A. Spates makes the following statement, and admits it to this record as the testimony of George W. McCulloh.

He was present when the tickets were counted out at Frost-burg District No. 5, and he thought the count was carefully and correctly made ; he did not examine or see the tickets, or keep a tally of the count made ; he can only speak from observation, having no personal knowledge.

T. A. OGLE, (Sworn.)
Interrogatory 1st, of schedule A.—T. A. Ogle, age 40 years, occupation saddler, residence in election District No. 6, in Allegany county, and have resided there 10 years.

Interrogatory 2d, as in schedule A. I was appointed, did qualify and act as such officer of Registration for the year 1866. I qualified before the Clerk of the Circuit Court for Allegany county. I had read the 'Constitution and laws relating registration. I did administer the oath ;to each and every one. I gave notice of the time and place of registration as required by law.

Interrogatory 3rd, as interrogatory 4, in schedule A.

(Excepted to by Mr. Spates.)

Answer. I did so enter. I did register some who had legal residence and were of lawful age, before said 1st day of November, 1865. I registered a great many of that kind ; C. W. Blengle, J. W. Jones, Dr. James M. Smith, J. B. Widner, G. B W. Rossee and others. I considered them entitled to register under the provisions of the registry law. I had no one's advice as to registering.

THEO. A. OGLE.

WILL. LOUDERMILK, (Sworn.)
Interrogatory 1st, as in schedule A. Will Lowdermilk. age 28 years, occupation publisher, residence in election District No. 13, of Allegany county, Maryland, have resided there 18 months.

Interrogatory 2d,. Did you publish the list of registered voters for any of the election Districts, of Allegany county, in

12

the year 1866 ; if so, who furnished you said list for publication, and at what time was it furnished ?

Answer. Yes, I published all of them ¿ they were furnished by different parties, Charles Scott, of Mt. Savage. furnished a list for District No. 12 ; he was officer of registration for that District. No other officer of registration furnished me lists for publication ; most all of them I got from the Alleganian ; and Mr. Spates furnished me with the list of District No. 5. which I refused to publish until he furnished Mr. Atkinson's signature. I published them in handbills : Mr. Atkinson was not with him when he furnished the list ; Mr. Atkinson was officer of registration and corrected the list. I printed the bills for Districts 7 and 8 ; can, t remember how I got said lists, but am satisfied I did not get them from the officer of registration ; I think Mr. Weber requested me to publish them as he could not do it in time.—The list of Mr. Scott was furnished long before time for publication ; they were published at a very late hour, but not positive that it was later than the time specified by law.

Interrogatory 3d. Have you in your office a file of the Civilian & Telegraph for the year 1864; if so. does said file show the publication of the findings and sentence of a Court Martial convicting Alfred Spates, of disloyal practices against the Government of the United States?

Excepted to by A. Spates.

Answer. I have the Civilian & Telegraph of the 16th of June, 1864, containing the charges and specifications, but not the findings and sentence of a military commission in the case referred to; and it also contains an order from the Major-General Commanding Department, directing the arrest and imprisonment of Mr. A. Spates in accordance with the sentence of that Court.

Answer excepted to by A. Spates.

First-Cross Interrogatory by A. Spates. How many newspapers were published in the year 1866, in Allegany county, and name them, and the publishers of each; and was the list of registered voters published in any other paper than the one published by yourself?

Answer. Three newspapers are published in Allegany county; the Alleganian by W. E. Weber; the Union by the Messrs Knorr's; the Civilian & Telegraph by myself. They were published in the Alleganian.

Second Cross-Interrogatory by A. Spates. Where did you reside in June 16, 1864; what was your occupation at said time, and where were you then stationed?

Answer. My residence at that time was in Louisville, Kentucky; I was in the United States army at that time; I was somewhere in the State of Georgia and returned to Allegany county in June, 1865.

Third Cross-Interrogatory. Were you in any way connected either as editor or publisher of the Civilian & Telegraph n the year 1864, or a subscriber to said paper; and did you at that time see a copy of said paper of the 16th of June in circulation, and when did you first become proprietor of said paper?

Answer. I was not in any way connected with it; I was not a subscriber, and only saw an occasional copy sent by a friend; I don't remember of seeing any of June 16, 1864; on the 1st day of July, 1865, I became proprietor of the Civilian & Telegraph   WILL H. LOUDERMILK.

Fourth Cross-Interrogatory by A. Spates. You say you have a copy of the Civilian & Telegraph of the 16th of June, 1864, containing charges and specifications but not the findings and sentence of a military commission; was the statement in the paper referred to, a certified copy of those proceedings, or was it an editorial?

Answer. It is from an editorial in that paper; that it is an editorial, and purports to quote from some other source the charges and specifications, with the order of the Major-General Commanding; source not given.

Interrogatory Fifth. Who wrote that editorial?

Answer. I was about twelve hundred miles from here about that time; I have no idea.

Interrogatory Sixth. Do you know from your own knowledge that there is a single statement in that editorial that is true?

Answer. I do not know from my own knowledge whether 'tis true or not true.

Interrogatory Seventh. If you believe that that editorial produced by you is evidence; which of the two do you think is the bigger fool, you or Dr. Ohr?

Answer. I have no answer to make.

Interrogatory Eighth. Who writes the editorials in the Civilian & Telegraph?

Answer. I write all the editorials for the Civilian & Telegraph; there are occasional articles handed me by other parties which appear as editorials.

Interrogatory Ninth. Who wrote those occasional articles: name them.

Answer. Dr. Ohr once gave me one article, and I published a part of it in an article of my own: probably a long time ago; may have been last Spring; cannot remember the time.

Interrogatory Tenth. In the Civilian & Telegraph of the 6th of September, 1866, now shown you, is an editorial, which speaks of the wives and concubines, and their sons wives and concubines, of the citizens who attended the barbacue at Cumberland on that day; did or did not Dr. Ohr write that article, if not, who did?

Answer. Dr. Ohr did not write it, did not see it or hear of it as far as I know of, until after the publication of the paper ; I wrote the article on the day before the publication, a few hours before going to press, and consulted no one in regard to it.

Cross Interrogatory No. 11.

Were the statements in that article true or not ? "This Interrogatory waved."

Cross Interrogatory No. 12.

Don't you know that the proceedings before the military commission spoken of were set aside by President Lincoln, who assigned as a reason by endorsement on the proceedings, that there was no evidence to sustain the charges ; and that the President dismissed the proceedings, and shortly thereafter, wrote a letter to the Board of Public Works of Maryland, requesting them to re-elect Mr. A. Spates as President of the Chesapeake and Ohio Canal Company, and which was accordingly done on the 3d of June, 1864 ?
Answer. I know nothing at all in regard to it.

Cross Interrogatory No. 13.

Do you not know that military commissions and military court-martials to try citizens in Maryland, not connected with the army and navy, were unconstitutional; their findings a nulity, and their findings prima facia evidence of wrong and falsehood.
Answer. I know nothing in regard to it.

Cross Interrogatory No. 14.

Are not the proceedings and evidence taken before the military commission spoken of in the editorial, of which you have testified, a matter of record in the archives of the Secretary of the War Department; and could not an authenticated copy of that record have been produced, to have shown what the findings were ; and do you not know that this record would have shown that the whole was a nulity, and set aside by the President as unsustained by evidence.
Answer. I have no personal knowledge in regard to the matter.

WILL H. LOUDERMILK.

Neither party desiring to make further interrogatories or producing other witnesses, I accordingly close this testimony, and certify that the foregoing is a true statement of answers given by the several witnesses as they were respectively produced and examined before me this day.

Given under my hand and seal this 29th day of December,
in the year of our Lord eighteen hundred and sixty-six.

J. M. STRONG, J. P. [SEAL.]

STATE OF MARYLAND,

ALLEGANY COUNTY, SET.

I hereby certify, that J. M. Strong, Esquire, before whom
the annexed affidavits were made, and whose genuine signature thereto appears, was, at the date thereof, a Justice of
the Peace in and for the State and county aforesaid, duly
commissioned and sworn, and authorized by law to administer oaths and take acknowledgments.

[SEAL.] In testimony whereof, I hereunto subscribe my
name and affix the seal of the Circuit Court for Allegany county, this 31st day of December, 1866.

H. RESLEY,
Clerk of the Circuit Court for Allegany county.

[United States 5 cent. stamp.]

Cross Interrogatories filed by Contestant.

Cross Interrogatory to R. W. Mason and H. R. Atkinson.

Cross Interrogatory 1. Did you receive a commission from
the Governor of Maryland, commissioning you to act as a Register in Allegany county ; if you did, did you take an oath for
the faithful performance of that duty before the Clerk of the
Circuit Court for Allegany county?

THOMAS J. McKAIG,
Attorney for A. Spates.

Cross Interrogatories filed by Contestant.

Cross Interrogatories to Wm. Conrad by A. Spates.

Cross Interrogatory 1. You say you saw the Clerks write
down the number of votes cast for Senator for C. H. Ohr and
A. Spates and returned the identical tickets to the Clerk's
office. Did you act as Return Judge for that district ; if you
did, did you and your fellow Judges make return of the number
of votes cast for each and every one voted for ; and did you,
as the Return Judge, make a true return of said election?

Interrogatory 2. Did you return by your return, any number of votes cast for Senator for C. H. Ohr or A. Spates ; if
yea, will you point out in your return what votes were cast
for C. H. Ohr, and how many were cast for A. Spates?

THOMAS J. McKAIG,
Attorney for A. Spates.

Cross Interrogatory to John Boward by Mr. Spates.

Cross Interrogatory 1. Was it possible while you were act-

94

ing as Judge and taking each ticket from the box and reading it before you handed it to your fellow Judge, to look over the ticket while the Judge read it, and to see that the Clerks put it down properly on the talies; how far from the talies did you sit; and were you close enough to read the names, and did you?

Cross Interrogatory 2. See every vote put down properly by the Clerks. When you and your fellow Judges counted the tickets over the second time, did you or did you not find a difference in the count from the first count made by you and the other two Judges; who were present when the second count was made; and why was it made; and when was it made, and how many times did you count them?

THOMAS J. McKAIG,
Attorney for A. Spates.

Cross Interrogatories to Joseph M. Koerner by Spates.

Cross Interrogatory 1. After the closing of the polls, did you and the other Judges carefully take out the said ballots and read distinctly and aloud, the name or names written or printed thereon respectively; or did you separate the tickets into what is called "straight-out" or whole tickets and "split tickets;" then mark down the whole tickets without reading out distinctly and aloud, each name on the ticket and tally them as such; and then did you read the "split tickets" and have them put down?

Cross Interrogatory 2. You say that Edward Williams voted at the polls at District No. 6, who had no right to vote because he was not a resident of No. 6; was his name on the list of registered voters for District No. 13, and to what party do you belong and for whom did you vote for State Senator?

THOMAS J. McKAIG,
Attorney for A. Spates.

Cross Interrogatories to be administered to James M. Matthews and John H. Stallings on the part of A. Spates.

Cross Interrogatory 1. You say John Diffenbaugh was registered as disloyal in 1865; did you take any testimony in regard to the disloyalty of the said Diffenbaugh; did he apply for registration; and did he take the oath required by the registers or did he refuse to take it; who were the witnesses against him and was he present at the time; what did you take down in writing as testified against him by the witnesses; and where is the testimony as taken down by you, can you produce it; if not, where is it; did you summon the witnesses and give notice that you were about to take up his case under charges against him?

THOMAS J. McKAIG,
Attorney for A. Spates.

Cross Interrogatories to be administered to Levi W. Brant by
A. Spates.

Cross Interrogatory 1. Did you and your fellow Judges read
every name on every ticket distinctly, or did you and your
fellow Judges separate the tickets into whole and split tickets;
if you did, did you read off the names of each name as printed
or written ; or did you simply say full ticket, naming the kind
of ticket; then did the Clerks put down a vote to each candidate on that ticket?

Cross Interrogatory 2. If the Judges and Clerks had acted
honestly, how could 653 tickets have got into the box when
you had only 643 names of voters ; or was it possible that the
Clerks may have omitted the names of some of the voters ?

MARYLAND,

ALLEGANY COUNTY, *to wit:*

I hereby certify, that the following entry appears on the
Books of Registration, in this office, for District No. 7, in
Allegany county, as returned by the Registers appointed by
the Governor for that District, in the year 1865. "John
Diffenbaugh, disloyalty under the 4th section of the 1st Ar-
ticle of the Constitution. Test : Michael Twigg, Thomas W.
Athy."

Witness my hand and official seal this 28th day of December, 1866.

[SEAL.]   H. RESLEY.
    Clerk of the Circuit Court for Allegany county, Md.

[United States 5 cent. stamp.]

For State Senator.

CHAS. H. OHR.   COL. ALFRED SPATES.
    (399.)   (296.)

I hereby certify, that the above is a true copy of the tally
of votes for State Senator, returned by Judges of Election
District number five (No. 5,) and now on file in the Clerk's
Office of Circuit Court for Allegany county, as taken from
the Poll Books for said District, at November election, 1866.

Witness my hand and official seal this 28th day of December, 1866.

[SEAL.]   H. RESLEY,
    Clerk of the Circuit Court for Allegany county, Md.

[United States 5 cent. stamp.]

TO THE PRESIDENT
OF THE SENATE OF MARYLAND.

STATE OF MARYLAND,
Allegany County, to wit :

I, Peter Baker, a Justice of the Peace of the State of Maryland, in and for Allegany county, duly commissioned and sworn, do hereby certify, that after application made to me by Charles H. Ohr, claimant of the office of Senator for Allegany county, I caused to be served on Alfred Spates, contestant of the election of said Ohr, as such Senator, notification, (a copy of which with the admission of service by said Alfred Spates, endorsed thereon, marked "Claimant's Exhibit C," hereunto annexed,) requiring him to attend at my office in Oakland, in said county, on the day and at the place specified in said notification, to cross-examine the witnesses therein named.

I further certify, that the witnesses whose depositions are herewith returned, begining on page 1, and continuing by consecutive pages to page 39, were first by me duly sworn to testify truly and fully in the matter of the contest referred to in the notification hereto attached; that I caused the testimony of the said witnesses together with the questions propounded by the parties, or their attorney, to be reduced to writing in my presence, and in the presence of the parties or their attorneys, by the witnesses themselves, or by John Gephart, who was first sworn, fairly to write down and transcribe the deposition of witnesses; that the deposition of each witness was taken down in pursuance thereof, and at the time and place mentioned in the notification aforesaid, that each witness signed his deposition in my presence, after the same had been read to him.

I further certify, the papers marked "Claimant's Exhibit C," was filed by the claimant on the date marked thereon.

PETER BAKER,   [SEAL.]

A Justice of the Peace for the State of Maryland,
in and for Allegany county.

STATE OF MARYLAND,

ALLEGANY COUNTY, *to wit:*

CUMBERLAND, December 17, 1866.

ALFRED SPATES,   ⎫

              ⎬ Contested Election for Senator from
vs.

CHARLES H. OHR. ⎭ Allegany county.

SIR: You are hereby notified in accordance with the provisions of Sections 57 and 59, of Article 35, of the Code of Public General Laws of Maryland, that an examination of the following witnesses, viz: J. Chisholm, Sr., G. S. Lee, Wm. R. Sollers, Upton F. Biggs, Isaac Thompson, Capt. Geo. W. Wilson, John W. Sollers, Wm. Harvey, N. B. Harvey, Noah Harvey, Middleton S. Biggs, James W. Harvey, John W. Lee, Jacob Abernathy, Alex. Kitzmiller, A. Chisholm, Jr., Daniel Chisholm, B. F. Harvey, Beckwith Shrout, John W. Irons, James W. White, Sam'l W. Friend, Wm. A. Falkenstine, Jonathan H. Wilson, Ebenezer Kitzmiller, Wm. Bray, M. G. Harvey, J. L. Browing, Phillip Doffert, Joseph Friend, H. B. Friend, John Riley, Wm. Hall, Wm. H. Hoye, Wm. W. Ashby, Henry Thompson, Henry Davis and Peter Baker, will take place at the office of Peter Baker, Esq., in the town of Oakland, Allegany county, Md, on Friday and Saturday, the 4th and 5th days of Jan., 1867, at 10 o'clock, A. M.; by these witnesses, Charles H, Ohr, expects to prove that the 1st, 2nd and 4th alledged grounds set forth in your notice of contest, are not true and did not occur, and that a number of illegal ballots were cast at the election held on the 6th day of November 1866, in Districts No. 1, 10 and 15, having thereon the name of Alfred Spates for State Senator.

If all the witnesses cannot be examined in the days named, then the examination to be continued from day to day, until it shall be completed.

You are required to attend at the above mentioned time and place, either in person or by attorney, for the purpose of cross-examining witnesses.

Given under my hand and seal, this 17th day of December, 1866.

                      PETER BAKER.   [SEAL.]

A Justice of the Peace of the State of Maryland,

                  in and for Allegany county.

I hereby certify, that I served a notice similar to the above upon Alfred Spates, at Cumberland, Allegany county, Maryland, on the 20th day of December, 1866.

                        G. M. RIZER.

13

Sworn to before me this 25th day of December, in the year of our Lord, eighteen hundred and sixty-six.

J. M. STRONG.   [SEAL.]

Justice of the Peace of the State of Maryland,

in and for Allegany county.

Interrogatories to be propounded for Charles H. Ohr, in case of A. Spates vs. C. H. Ohr.

SCHEDULE A.

OAKLAND, MD., January 4th and 5th.

Interrogatorry 1st. What is your name, age, occupation and residence and how long have you lived there?

Interrogatory 2d. Did you receive from the Governor the appointment of officer of registration for said election district; did you qualify and act as such and for what year, had you read the Constitution and law regulating the registration of voters, before entering on the discharge of that duty, did you administer the "oath of voters," asprescribed in Article 1st, section 4th, of the Constitution of Maryland, to each person before entering his name in the eighth column of the book of registration, or on the list of qualified voters, and did you give notice as required by law of the times and places of registration?

Interrogatory 3d. Did you or did you not enter in the eighth column of the book of registration, or on the list of qualified voters for said District, the names of persons whose names had previously been entered or registered as disloyal; if so, state your reasons and authority for so doing fully and in detail and give the names of the persons so entered and with which political party do they act?

Interrogatory 4th. Did you enter on your said book of registration any names not before entered and register them as qualified voters; if so, were they persons who were of lawful age, and had legal residence in said District before the 1st day of November, 1865, if so, give your reasons and authority for so doing; name the persons and the political party with which they act?

Interrogatory 5th. Was your name registered as a voter before the 1st day of August, 1866; did you vote for State

Senator at the election on the 6th day of November, 1866 ; if so, for whom did you so vote ?

Interrogatory 6th. Were the polls for your District held at the place advertised or published by the sheriff, and was the election as quiet and orderly as usual at said polls ?

———

Interrogatories to be propounded for C. H. Ohr, in the contested election of Spates vs. Ohr.

SCHEDULE B.

Interrogatory 1st. What is your name, age, occupation residence, and time of such residence ?

Interrogatory 2d. Did you receive the appointment as judge of election for said District in 1866; did you qualify and act as such on the 6th day of November, 1866; did the judges of said election make public a declaration that all persons registered in 1866, would by them be required to take the "oath of voters," as prescribed in Article 1st section 4th of the Constitution of Maryland; if so, for what reason, and did the said judges of election have armed men stationed at the doors or windows of the place where the polls were held or authorize them to be so stationed; if so, for what reason ?

Interrogatory 3d. Did you as judges of said election, refuse or reject the ballot tendered by any person whose name appeared on the list of qualified voters, unconditionally and peremptorily and without requiring them to take any oath; if so, whom and for what reason ?

Interrogatory 4th. Did you see or hear any violence intimidation or threats, used by any person or persons to deter or intimidate persons from offering to vote ; if so who used the intimidation and who was so prevented, and to what political party do they belong; was the election on the 6th of November last, as quiet and orderly as usual at your said polls !

Interrogatory 5th. Is it not customary for the people of your District to carry their guns with them to public gatherings, more particularly at that season of the year, and was there an unusual display of guns at your polls; if so, state the reasons fully and whether the armed men belonged to one or both political parties, as also their names?

Interrrogatory 6th. Did you hear any discharge of fire arms on the day of said election near the polls; if so, under what circumstances, in what manner and by whom ?

Interrogatory 7th. Did you vote for State Senator on the 6th of November, 1866; if so, for whom did you so vote; were the polls held at the place published by the sheriff for that purpose; how far is it from the Virginia line; and how far do you reside from the place were the polls were held?

TESTIMONY.

(Excepted to as not in the notice, by A. Spates.)

SAMUEL W. FRIEND, sworn.

Interrog. 1st. As No. 1 in schedule A.

Samuel W. Friend; age 55 years; occupation farmer; residence, Election District No. 1, Allegany county, Maryland; have resided there 19 years.

Interrog. 2d. As No. 2 in schedule A.

I was appointed, I qualified and acted as such for the year 1865. I had read the law and Constitution. I did. I gave notice as required by law.

Interrog. 3d. Did the officers enter on said book the names of any persons as disqualified under the provisions of the Constitution; if so, name them?

Answer. Yes; we aimed to do so. We entered Henry Hamill in the 7th column as disqualified, and Randolph Beckman, and we entered Alexander Farall and William Reinhart as disqualified for refusing to take the oath; also Patrick Hamill, as generally known as disloyal, but did not enter the testimony; George O'Brien as disloyal, as giving aid and comfort. I think there were more, but do not recollect them.

Interrog. 4. As No. 2 in schedule B.

I received the appointment. I qualified and acted as such. No, not all persons, were informed by public notice that they would be required to take the oath. We had no armed men at the polls, and did not authorize any, and there were none there.

Interrog. 5. As No. 3 in schedule B.

No, not a single man. We did not refuse any man's vote without requiring them to take the oath.

Interrog. 6. As No. 7 in schedule B.

I voted for Dr. Ohr for State Senator. The polls were held at the place as published by law, by the Sheriff.

Cross Interrogations by A. Spates.

Interrog. 1. Did you give the persons whom you, as Register, in 1865, entered as disloyal and disqualified, notice to appear when their case was to be investigated, confront them with the witnesses against them, and record said testimony in the registry book, with rebutting evidence, if any was furnished, and were such witnesses summoned to appear then ?

Answer. We gave the notice as required by law. We did not give them personally a notice. The witnesses were present and they were sworn, and had been summoned. Against Henry Hamill was Silas Fitzwater, Samuel Friend and Abraham Hershburger. Henry Hamill did not appear at any time; did not leave a notice upon him to appear; he did not apply to me for registration; we did not administer to him the constitutional oath, because he did not appear before us. Against Randolph Beckman the witness was Benjamin Davis; he was not there when the testimony was given in by Davis; he came afterwards and the testimony was read over to him, and he acknowledged that it was right. He did not vote at the election held on the 6th of November, 1866; he did not offer to vote. Against Alexander Farall there appeared no witnesses; he refused to take the oath, and said he would not take it. He was entered in the 7th column as disqualified.

Cross interrogatory 2d. Was the entry for disqualification against Mr. Farall made in accordance with the Constitution and Registry Law, you having stated in the examination in chief that you had read both ?

Answer. I aimed to so enter it, to the best of my judgment.

Interrog. 3d. Did Mr. Farall vote in 1866 ?

Answer. I think he did not; he refused to take the oath.

Interrog. 4th. Did you or not first refuse his vote, before requiring him to take the oath ?

Answer. Mr. Kitzmiller said, Mr. Farall, your vote is challenged; you must come in and take the oath.

Interrog. 5. Was that remark made at the time he offered his vote ?

Answer. It was made at the time he presented his vote.

Interrog. 7th. What answer did Mr. Farall make to the declaration of Mr. Kitzmiller ?

I don't recollect his exact words, but gave us to understand that he would not take the oath.

Interrog. 8th. What oath did you offer him.

Answer. The Constitutional oath.

Interrog. 9. Did William Reinhardt vote, or offer to vote, November 6th, 1866 ?

Answer. He did not.

Interrog. 10th. Did Patrick Hamill vote or offer to vote?

Answer. He did not vote, but offered to vote; his vote was rejected; he refused to take the oath when he tendered his vote; he afterward took the oath in the evening, but did not then offer his vote, and refused to answer any questions. Mr. Hamill did not appear before us in 1865 to register; the entry, I think, made against him was generally disloyal; there was testimony against him, but never recorded; if I recollect right it was a violation of the 4th section of the Constitution, Article 1st.

Interrog. 11th. Was that entry made on the book of registration ?

Answer. Not in that way; the entry that was made was, generally known to be disloyal, under the circumstances we thought that that was as good a way as any to enter it.

Interrog. 12th. What were the charges against George O'Brien; and was he before you for registration ?

Answer. They were that he furnished a horse for Thos. West to go South; and that he harbored and fed Hiram Tasker, Charles West and others on their return from the South; according to my recollection he was before me for registration.

Interrog. 13th. Do you know, of your own knowledge, whether these charge are true or false ?

Answer. The charge of having fed West and Tasker on their return from the South, he told me was true, but that he did not know it was wrong. I do not know that he furnished the horse, exceept by the testimony that appeared before me as Register.

Interrog. 14. Where is that testimony; if you have it, produce it ?

Answer. Affidavit of Phillip Doffert, produced and filed, marked exhibit S. W. Friend.

GEO. O'BRYAN,
To PHILLIP DOFFERT, Dr.

Aug. 24, 1862,   To a Mare, Saddle and Bridle $75.00

(See Interrogatory 14th, Page 7.)

STATE OF MARYLAND,

ALLEGANY COUNTY, to wit:

Personally appeared before me, the subscriber, a Justice of the Peace in and for said county, Joseph Miller, who after being duly sworn according to law, says and declares on his oath, that Geo. O'Brian told him, the said Joseph Miller, on the Evening of the 24th of August last, that he, the said, Geo. O'Brian, "had promised and pledged his word and honor to see Philip Doffert paid for his mare, if he would let Thos. West have the Mare." I heard the said Geo. O'Brian, repeat several times afterwards that he had promised his word and honor, and would see Phillip Doffert paid for the mare; and I know that the said Doffert never would have given the mare without this repeated promise of Geo. O'Bryan, to see him paid for the mare, and therefore, the above sum of seventy-five dollars, is justly due to the said Philip Doffert.

Sworn before

J. M. STRONG,
Justice of the Peace.

April 2, 1863.

August 30, 1865.

I, Philip Doffert, do on oath state that in the Fall of 1862, Thomas West and others, came to my House, and on the same evening I was called away on business belonging to family affairs; when, on the day following, I was at Mrs. Broberts, and my wife came down and said: "the party had left and taken my mare along with them." In the evening, George O'Bryan met me on my road home, and said: "I will pay you for your mare if Truman West don't." And at different times afterwards told me to the same effect. About the number collected at my house to go South, I think was five, these parties some I know and some I did not know.

SAML. W. FRIEND,
Register at Altamont.

PHILIP DOFFERT.

Interrog. 14. Look upon the paper shown you marked S. W. Friend, and state whose hand writing it is, before whom is it sworn to, and by what authority had the party signing, to administer said oath?

Answer. In my hand writing; sworn before me as Register, appointed by the Governor of the State of Maryland, date August 30, 1865, and taken in the office of registration; Mr. O'Brien was not present when this affidavit was made.

Interrog. 15. Whose names were on the list of the parties to be challenged at the polls, and who furnished said list?

Answer. P. Hammill, H. O. Hammill, Henry Hammill, Sr., Archibald Hammill, Alexander Farrall, Richard J. West, Reason Turner, and Geo. O'Brian; it was furnished by E. Blackburn, Hagans, J. L. Browning and others.

Interrog. 16 Did you, or not, publicly declare before said election, that certain parties who were registered in 1866, should not vote; and had you a list of said persons at the polls.

Answer. I have no recollection of making such a declaration, I had a list of eight persons handed me at the polls, before any votes were taken.

Interrog. 17. Did you, or either of the Judges of Election call any person or persons in side the poll room, and there or at any other place, solicit him or them, to vote the Radical ticket.

Answer. To the best of my knowledge it was not done.

Interrogatory 19th. Were the names of the 8 persons on the list furnished you and above spoken of, also on the registration list of 1866 as qualified voters which was furnished you by the register of your district on the day of election?

Answer. I think they were; I think none of the eight voted.

Interrogatory 20th. If those eight persons, or either of them, had taken the oath you offered, would you then, without any questioning, have received their votes?

Answer. Some of them I would not, but in the case of A. C. Hammil, had he appeared before me and taken the oath, I would, as I advised him to take the oath; also, in the case of Reason Turner; I would, but he said he had never taken the oath, nor never would, had they answered all questions satisfactorily, and there had been no evidence against them, I would have received their votes.

S. W. Friend, re-examined by Dr. Ohr. Did any of the persons registered by you in 1865, as disqualified, vote at the election in November, 1866, if so, how many, and with what political party do they act?

Answer. I do not think any voted that I registered as disqualified.

SAMUEL W. FRIEND.

(Excepted to by A. Spates.)

Wm. Harvey, (Sworn):

Interrogatory 1st. As No. 1 in Schedule B.

Answer. Wm. Harvey, age 61 years, occupation farmer, residence election district No. 10 of Allegany county, resided there not quite one year, say 11 months.

Interrogatory 2nd, as No. 4 in Schedule B.

Answer. I did not to my recollection.

Interrogatory 3rd, as No. 6 in Schedule B.

I heard no discharge of fire arms about the polls, but after a good many of them, (the Conservatives) got about two hundred yards from the polls down the lane, I heard the discharge of fire arms; some of those who left in the party Wm. Kitzmiller, Wm. Arnold, Jas. F. Liller, George M. Mosser and others, saw twenty.

Interrogatory 4, as No. 7 in Schedule B.

I voted for Charles H. Ohr for State Senator; I believe they were three miles from the Virginia State line, at least eight miles from where the polls were held.

First Cross-interrogatory by A. Spates.

Did either of the parties mentioned in your answer to interrogatory 3d, viz: Jas. F. Liller, Wm. Kitzmiller, Wm. Ar-

14

nold, Geo. M. Mosser and say the twenty more or less, vote on that day?

Answer. I am not able to say whether any of them did or did not; I think the most of them did not.

Interrogatory 2d. Did any of the said parties mentioned have arms with them at the polls; how many, and who, and how do you know they were Conservatives?

Answer. They did; I cannot recollect how many; Liller had a gun, and I think Mosser as well as Arnold, but I will not be positive about it; they called themselves Democrats and I heard some of them say that they wanted to vote that ticket.

Interrogatory 3d. Did you see any persons who called 'themselves Radicals or Unionists, at the polls with arms, and how many, and did all such vote.

Answer. I did, I don't remember how many, say from 5 to to 12, they all did as far as I know, at least the most of them did I think.

Excepted to by A. Spates.

WM. HARVEY.

Geo. W. Willson, (Sworn.)
Interrogatory 1st. As No. 1, in Schedule B. G. W. Willson, age 30 years; occupation, farmer; residence district No. 10, of Allegany county, Maryland, have resided there 7 years.

Interrogatory 2d. As 4 in Schedule B.

Answer. I did not more so than usual.

Interrogatory 3d. As 5 in Schedule B.

Answer. It is custumary for the people of my district to carry their guns to public gatherings, more particularly at that season of the year, I cannot say whether there was a display of more guns than usual, perhaps there was; it had been currently reported for two or three months, that the Conservatives were coming there to break up the election and the ballot box, unless they were permitted to vote, and that there was to be a party from West Virginia to assist them, it was stated that Wm. Kitzmiller had written a letter to Petersburg, and that they expected a party of roughs from there, there was a protracted meeting at Ryans' Glades, some three or four weeks before the election, a party came there from West Union and Chisholm's Mill, in West Virginia. They came there at an unusual hour, one of them had fire arms, and they commenced fighting, but don't know which party commenced it, they were whipped out at the religious meeting, and then said they would have satisfaction at the polls, a part of them had been in McNeal's gurrilla company of the Confederate Army; Wm. Hoye, of Md., Wallace Chisholm, Peter Chisholm, the two Chisholms live in West Virginia, and a young man by the name of Mason, from West Virginia; I was clerk on the day of election, and could not see the armed men.

1st Cross-Interrogatory by A. Spates.

Are you well acquainted in West Virginia, near Chisholm's Mill and West Union.

Answer. I am only partially acquainted, I suppose there was between twenty and thirty-five guns at the polls on the 6th of November, 1866, the Conservative party had left before I came out, and there was that many I saw, when I did come out; I have seen at previous elections, as many guns as at that one, at the first election of Lincoln, I saw as many guns in the year of 1860; I have no personal knowledge of the truth of the rumors, as testified to by me about a party coming from West Virginia, or a letter written by Wm. Kitzmiller, to Petersburg, about a Conservative party going to break up the polls and ballot box, among the party who came to Ryan's Glade, at the time of the protracted meeting, Wm. Hoye was the only armed one that I know of, about mid-day when they came, and the service was over, I did not hear them make the threats about making it all right at the polls, nor do I know that they were in the Confederate Army, except by heresay.

Cross-Interrogatory 2d. Was there an organized, armed company at the polls Novemver 6th, 1866, in District No. 10?

Answer. There was a sort of an organized company; it was organized at a meeting held at Ryan's Glades a week or two previous to the election, by the citizens of the district; Benj. F. Harvey was elected Captain, 1st Lieut. Jas. W. White, in organizing the company, we selected such men for officers as we thought would keep one party from interfering with the opposite political party, as well to resist an attack should we be attacked by a party from West Virginia, as we were threatened, it was a cautionary measure.

Interrog'y 3d. Was there or not, by a resolution passed at the meeting, a certain number of persons then named, to go to the polls on the day of election with arms, for the protection of the judges of election?

Answer. There was not.

Cross-Interrogatory 4th. Was or was not an armed force at the polls on the day of election?

Answer. There were men there with arms.

Cross-Interrogatory 5th. State the object of those men being there armed, and the name of each person so armed, as far as you can recollect; and had you, yourself arms there on that day?

Answer. It was in accordance with the general custom and to resist an attack, as it was rumored we were to be at, tacked that day; Benj. Harvy, Jas. W. Harvy, Wm. Wilson, Archibald Chisholm, Beckwith Shrout, and I think Wm. Riggs, Chas. Lish, James W. White, and I had a pistol, the parties that I named belonged to the Union party, the window was chiefly occupied by the Conservatives, I saw nine stationed about, there was thirteen Conservative votes cast there that day, and sixty-nine Union.

Cross-Interrogatory No. 6th. State, if you know, how many votes were refused there that day?

Answer. Did not take any notice, suppose that there were 20 more or less, that belonged to the Conservative party principally. (So I supposed.)

Cross-Interrogatory 7th.

Did you or did you not just previous to the election, receive by railroad and directed to you at Oakland, supplies for the use of the company which the citizens organized at a meeting in District No. 10, to attend the polls on the day of election.

Answer. Yes there was a lot of bread and meat, and a keg of beer was sent out for a dinner at the polls.

GEORGE W. WILSON.

(Excepted to by A. Spates.)

WM. H. HALL, (Sworn.)

Interrogatory 1. As No. 1, in schedule A.

Answer. Wm. H. Hall, age 45 years, occupation farmer, residence District No. 15, Allegany county, Maryland, resided there 10 years.

Interrogatory 2. As 2 in schedule A.

Answer. I received such an appointment, I qualified and acted as such for the year 1866. I had read the Law and Constitution regulating the registration of voters before entering upon said duties; I did administer the oath as prescribed before entering the name in the 8th column of said book; I gave notice as required by law of the time and place of registration.

Interrogatory 3rd. As No. 3, in schedule A. I believe I did in one or two instances, Mr. Peter Brant and Nelson Baker had been put down as having been in the rebel army, and the registers of 1865, said it was a mistake, and requested me to allow them to correct it, and I registered them.

Interrogatory 4th. As 4th in schedule A. I registered 59 or 60, some of which came of age since November 1865; say 3 or 4, I suppose the majority could have registered in 1865, if they had desired to, I was guided solely by the register law.

Interrogatory 5th. As 5 in schedule A.

Answer. My name was registered as a voter before the 1st of August 1866; and I voted for A. Spates for State Senator.

Interrogatory 6th. Did you after the Confederate forces had entered Oakland, give that information to Truman West and his daughter, at the house of said West; and what was the purport of your information and conversation on that occasion.

(Excepted to by A. Spates.)

Answer. I was through the neighborhood after the Confederates had been here, but I do not recollect, that I was in West's house or had any conversation with him about the matter, merely mentioned it as general news, I might have mentioned it.

W. H. HALL.

(Excepted to by A. Spates.)

GEO. S. LEE, (Sworn.)

Interrogatory 1. As 1, in schedule A. G. S. Lee, age 40 years, occupation farmer, residence No. 10 District, Allegany county, Maryland, have resided there about 17 years.

Interrogatory 2. As 2, in schedule A.

Answer. I did receive the appointment and did qualify, and act as such for 1865; I had read the law and Constitution regulating registration, and administered the oath to all whom appeared for same, and gave notice as to the time and place of registration.

Interrogatory 3rd. As 2, in schedule B. I did and qualified and acted as such, I do not know that we did make a public declaration, that all persons registered in 1866, would be required to take the oath of the Constitution of Article 1, section 4, there were no armed men stationed about the polls by our authority?

Interrogatory 4. As 3, in B. We did refuse, we refused McClure Mason, David S. Arnold, Charles O. Nethkin and Charles Best, Jacob Shaffer, Benjaman F. Shaffer and John Whorral, because they were proven disloyal in 1865, before the registers.

Interrogatory 5. As 4 in Schedule B. I saw no violence whatever ; it was quiet, as usual, at our polls.

Interrogatory 6. As 5, in Schedule B. It is customary to carry the guns to the polls ; I don't think that there was an unusual display of guns at the polls on that day ; I saw them there belonging to both parties ; I think it was from the threats that had been made to break up the election ; the report was that at a meeting sometime during the summer, the speakers said they should all vote or break the ballot box on the Judges heads or at the point of the bayonet ; Thomas J. McKaig, was one of the speakers, the information came from James Bradford a Conservative, it was current all the summer afterwards.

Interrog. 7. as 7, in Schedule B. I voted for Chas. H. Ohr for State Senator; the poles were held at the usual place in our district, about 3 or 3½ miles from the Virginia line; I reside 12 or 13 miles from where the polls were held; says that Dr. Ohor, did not advise any resistance in speech made in district No 10.

1st Cross-Interrogatory by Mr. Spates.

Did you or not notify J. McGlure Mason, David S. Arnold, Chas. O. Nethkin, Chas. Best, Jacob Shaffer, B. F. Shaffer add John Whorral, to appear before you in 1865; when you were register; that their cases would be diposed of; and did they appear and confront the witnesses at the time appointed by you; did they take the constitutional oath, or apply for registration in 1865, were their names upon the list as qualified voters, furnished you by the Register, November 6th, 1866.

Answer. We did not notify them in person, we only gave the general notice; they did not appear; they did not apply for registration in 1865, and did not take the constitutional oath; I think they were upon the list.

Cross-Interrogatory by A. Spates.

The reports you speak of, that the Conservatives would attack the polls on election day; and that Thos. J. McKaig had advised to vote at the point of the Bayonet; or break the ballot-box over the judges heads, and such like rumors; do you know any thing of your own knowledge of their truth or falsity, or did you only hear it rumored?

Answer. I only heard it rumored, I know nothing of my own knowledge. '

Cross-interrogatory 3d.

How many Conservative votes were polled, and how many rejected in District No. 10, November 6th, 1866; 13 polled, and 8 rejected on the ground of disloyalty, and dont remember how many on other grounds; the others could have, had they taken the oath.

Cross-interrogatory 4th.

Have you been sued by several persons for refusing their votes at the election on the 6th of November, 1866?

Answer. We have been sued by some 14.

Interrogatory 5th. Before whom did you qualify as Register in 1865; and did you file a list of the qualified voters registered by you in 1865, with the Clerk of the Circuit Court for Allegany county, as required by the Registry Law.

Answer. Before a Justice of the Peace, not in person; we made out one, and started it; but dont know what became of it; we gave it to Jas. Chisholm, Sr., for delivery to the Clerk of the Circuit Court; and Chisholm states he does not know what became of it.

GEORGE S. LEE.

(Excepted to by A. Spates.)

EBENEZER KITSMILLER, (Sworn.)

Interrog. 1. as 1 in Schedule B. E. Kitzmiller; my age, 44 years; occupation, manufacturer; residence, Election District No. 1. in Allegany county, Md.; and have resided there 19 years.

Interrog. 2. as 2 in Schedule B.

Answer. Was so appointed; did qualify and act as such; not until they came to the polls.

Interrog. 3. as 3 in Schedule B. There was two; Henry Hammill and Geo. O'Brian, because there was testimony against them; that they were disloyal.

Interrog. 4. Did you hear of any persons advising resisttance to the action of the Judges of Election, or threats of violence, in case of refusal of votes by the Judges of Election; if so, state fully where and by whom?

Answer. I did not; I did not hear any body say so, myself.

1st Cross-interrogatory by A. Spates.

What was the testimony against Hammill and O'Brian; and by whom was it furnished?

Answer. Of giving the Rebels bread and meat on a raid; and he refused to take the oath on an election; dont know what one; this testimony was furnished by S. W Friend.

2d Cross Interrog. Did you or any of the Judges of Election, on November 6th, 1866, solicit any person or persons to vote at said election; and was Samuel W. Friend a Judge of Election in District No. 1 on that day?

Answer. We did not; he was.

3d Cross Interrog. Did you hear S. W. Friend request and advise Rezin Turner and A. C. Hamill to take the oath and vote on that day?

Answer. I did.

EBENEZER KITZMILLER.

J. L. BROWNING, sworn.

Interrog. 1. As No. 1 in schedule A.

J. L. Browning; age 38 years; occupation, farmer; residence in Election District No. 1, of Allegany county, Maryland; resided there 3 years.

Interrog. 2. Did you furnish any names to the Judges of Election, held November 6th, 1866, as those of illegal voters; if so, whom, and what were your reasons for so doing; state them fully?

I furnished two names, those of George O'Brien and Richard J. West; I have heard O'Brien say that he furnished Hiram Tasker provisions on their return from the Southern lines; they were about O'Brien's premises and he furnished them provisions; say two or three meals.

1st Cross Interrogatory by A. Spates.

What amount of provisions did O'Brien furnish Tasker and West, and do you know that they were Confederate soldiers?

Answer. Gave them two or three meals; I don't know of my own knowledge whether they were Confederate soldiers or not.

2d Cross Interrog. Do you know whether the names of R. J. West and George O'Brien were on the list furnished the Judges by the Register, November 6, 1866?

Answer. I do not; I never saw the list.

JAMES L. BROWNING.

(Excepted to by A. Spates.)

JOHN W. IRONS.

Interrog. 1. As No. 1 in schedule A.

J. W. Irons; age 20 years; occupation farmer; residence in Election District No. 10, Allegany county, Maryland; have lived there 8 months.

Interrog. 2. Did you attend the polls of said district, on the 6th of November last; did you see any armed men at the polls, and to what political party did they belong; did you see or hear any violence, intimidation, or threats used to prevent persons from offering their votes?

Answer. I was there on the day of election; I saw armed men there of both parties; I did not.

Interrog. 3d. Did you hear any conversation among the Conservatives in regard to voting at said election; if so, what was it, and give their names?

Answer. I did; an old man by the name of Phillips and Wallace Chisholm and others; the old man advised their party to leave the polls and not try to vote, because it was not worth while to try to vote; to let the Judges be, that they would all be sorry for it, and that it was no use to try to do anything, for the party was too strong for them, but that there would be another time.

Interrog. 4. Were these armed men, and how?

Answer. Phillips, as far as I saw, had only a hickory club; I saw McMason's son have a revolver; yes, he was in and out among them, there was also Henry Ritter, who I am certain had a revolver, and I saw others there with rifles, but I do not remember their names.

1st Cross Interrogatory by A. Spates.

Did you vote, or offer to vote?

Answer. I did not vote, or offer to vote.

2d Cross Interrog. What were you doing at the polls?

Answer. I went with a party, because I understood there was a Rebel party coming there to storm the polls; to see what was to come off and to protect and keep peace.

3d Cross Interrog. Were you armed, and how; were those with whom you went armed, and how many were they; and to what party did you all belong?

Answer. I had a Springfield rifle; all the party I went with had arms, some six or seven in number; we all belonged to the Radical party.

4th Interrog. How many Conservatives did you see armed that day, and did you count them?

Answer. I saw Henry Ritter, A. Mason and several others, whose names I don't know, there, armed.

5th Cross Interrog. How do you know that they were Conservatives; and were they voters in District No. 10?

Answer. By hearing them talking; I heard them say they were Conservatives, and that they did not care who knew it; they were about ten or fifteen paces distant from me; to the best of my knowledge; Ritter and Mason I did not hear say anything; I think they live in District No. 10; I don't know whether they voted, or were registered, the club Phillips had was about one inch thick or more, and three and a half feet long; hickory wood, to the best of my knowledge; the bark was on it.

6th Cross Interrog. Under whose control were you and your party; who were your Captain and Lieutenant?

Answer. We called Benjamin Harvey Captain; some called J. W. White Lieutenant.

(Excepted to by Mr. Spates.)

Jas. W. White, (Sworn.)

Interrogatory 1, No. 1, in schedule B. James W. White, age 27 years, occupation farmer, residence election District No. 10, in Allegany county, resided there 27 years.

Interrogatory 2, as 4, in schedule B. I did not hear any threats or see any violence used at the election; the election was as quiet and orderly as any that I have ever attended.

Interrogatory 3, as 5, in schedule B. It is customary to carry guns to the election, to hunt Deer, but I believe there

15

was an unusual number of guns at the polls that day, and
they were carried by both parties ; there were rumors of
threats used by the Conservative party, that they would have
their votes or break the ballot-box over the judges heads, and
that men from West Va., would aid them in this work, and
to resist the attack from men in West Va. ; men carried their
arms to the election.

Intrrrogatory 4, as, 6, in schedule B. I heard the discharge
of fire-arms in or about two hundred yards from the polls; the
men that belonged to the Conservative party went away
from the polls in a body (at least a majority did) and after
leaving the polls some 15 to 40 shots were fired ; they were
fired by the men of the Conservative party, I suppose to show
us that they had fire-arms ; there was one or two men with
them who had served in the rebel army, and who was said to
have been in McNeil's guerilla company.

1st Cross Interrogatory, by A Spates. Do you know any
thing of your own knowledge as to the truth of the rumors
you have spoken of ; and if so, state what it is.

Answer. I know nothing of my own knowledge of the truth
of these rumors.

2d Cross interrogatory. Give the names of the persons who
fired the shots about two hundred yards from the polls ; and
state how you know them to be Conservatives.

Answer. Don't know their names. I knew it by their talk
and the company they keep; because they were in company
with WallaceChisholm, and John Phillips, and I heard them
talking that day, saying that the judges of election wanted to
crush the Democratic party. Wallace Chisholm lives in
Virginia.

3d Cross-interrogatory. Did you attend the election that
day ; were you armed and how ; how many were there armed,
and to what party did they belong?

Answer. I attended the election and was armed with a
double barrelled shot-gun, having only two charges; there was
8 of us went to the polls together, and all armed but one,
and we belong to the Radical party ; besides these, we found
when we got there some 10 more ; I don't know how many
Conservatives were there armed ; three or four I know were
armed with guns that I suppose belonged to the Conservative
party.

4th Cross-interrogatory. Were you in any manner recog-
nized as an officer of an armed body or party, for the purpose
of attending the polls November 6, 1866, the day of election ?

Answer. I decline to answer that question.

5th Cross-interrogatory. Were you appointed or elected
as Lieutenant of an armed party to attend the polls on elec-
ion day, November 6th, 1866 ?

Answer. I believe I was elected as such.

6th Interrogatory. Did you so attend the polls ?
Answer, I decline to answer.

JAMES W. WHITE.

(Excepted to by A. Spates.)

WILLIAM R. SOLLARS, (Sworn.)
Interrogatory 1. as No. 1, in B. Wm. R. Lollers, my age
50, occupation farmer, residence in Election District No. 10,
Allegany county, Maryland, have lived there 7 years.

Interrogatory 2, as 2, in B.

Answer. I was so appointed ; did qualify and act for 1865;
had read the Constitution and law before entering upon that
duty ; did so administer the oath ; I did give notice.

Interrogatory 3. Did you register any persons as disqualified for disloyalty ; if so name them.

Answer. William Wilderson, John Knepp, Rob't Lee,
Wm. Moon, Wm. H. Kitzmiller, J. M. Shaffer Henry Shaffer, David S. Arnold, J. McClure Mason and John Phillips, I
don't know whether any of the above named voted at the last
election or not ; some of them were published as registered.

1st Cross-interrogatory by A. Spates.

Before whom did you qualify as Register in 1855 ?

Answer. Before squire Baker.

2d Cross-interrogatory. Did the parties whom you mentioned as disqualified from voting in 1865, apply to you to
be registered ?

Answer. They did ; we did not administer the Constitutional oath because they did not appear.

3d Cross-interrogatory. Did you give them notice that their
cases would be investigated, and were they present to confront the witnesses against them, when you so registered
them as disqualified ?

Answer. We simply gave the ordinary notice ; they did
not appear.

4th Cross-interrogatory. Did you make a return of the
registered voters in District No. 10, for 1865, to the Clerk of
the Circuit Court for Allegany county ?

Answer. We thought we had.

Fifth Cross-interrogatory. How many of the persons marked by you as disloyal in 1865, voted at the election, Nov. 6,
1866.

Answer. I did not see any of them vote.

WILLIAM R. SOLLARS.

(Excepted to by A. Spates.)

JAMES CHISHOLM, Sr.

Interrogatory No. 1, as 1 in B.

James Chisholm age 65, years, occupation miller, residence
Election District, No. 10, in Allegany county, Md., have lived
there 17 years.

Interrogatory 2, as in B.

Was so appointed and did qualify and act; we told them as they came forward to vote; I did not have armed men stationed.

Interrogatory 3. Did you receive the votes at said election of Wm. Wilderson, John Kuepp, Robt. Lee,*Wm. Moon. and John M. Shaffer; if so did they take the oath of voters as prescribed in Article 1st, section 4, at your polls, on said day.

Answer. We did receive the vote of Wm. Wilderson, and he took the oath, and Robt. Lee, voted and took the oath; Wm. Moon did not vote; I don't think either Knepp or Kitzmiller voted.

Interrogatory 4th. Did you refuse to take the vote of Henry Thompson, and did you or not require him to take the oath of voters before you refused his vote?

Answer. We refused his vote because he refused to take the oath ; we told him that there was no charges against him, and if he would take the oath he could vote.

1st Cross-interrogatory, by A. Spates. Were the names mentioned in the third interrogatory on the registry list as qualified voters, which was furnished you by the register for District No. 10, November 6th, 1866 ?

Answer. They were on the list furnished by the register.

2d Cross-interrogatory. Did you or not refuse Henry Thompson's vote, and then tell him if he would take the oath that he could vote, as there were no charges against him ?

Answer. We called him inside and made this statement ; I think he offered his vote on the outside and we called him in.

3d Cross-interrogatory. Did you attend any meeting in which an armed force was organized or proposed to be organized, for the purpose of attending the polls on the day of election, in District No. 10, November 6th, 1866 ?

Answer. I was at such; there was a proposition made for a few men to come there and protect the judges in the pursuance of their duties; I suppose they did attend; the continual rumors caused us to form said party for protection of the judges and ballot-boxes, which was the reason I encouraged its forming; the proposition was enforced and carried out.

Fourth Cross-Interrogatory. Apprehending danger, did you apply to the Sheriff of the county to protect the judges in the discharge of their duty on the day of election, November 6th, 1866 ?

Answer. I did not.

Fifth Cross-Interrogatory. Do you not know that it was a violation of the law for the judges of election, of which you were one, to hold an election within two miles of any armed force?

Answer. I did not.

Sixth Cross-Interrogatory. Do you not know that it was a

violation of the law, for you, as one of the judges of election, to participate in organizing an armed force to attend the polls on the day of election?

Answer. I do not know what the law says on that head.

Seventh Cross-Interrogatory. Have any suits been brought against you for refusing to receive votes at the election held in District No. 10, Allegany county, Md., Nov. 6, 1866; if so, how many?

Answer. There are so many I cannot recollect.

Eighth Cross-Interrogatory. How many Radical and how many Conservative votes were polled in District No. 10, at the election held November 6th, 1866?

Answer. To the best of my knowledge sixty-nine Radical votes were polled, and thirteen Conservatives.

JAMES CHISHOLM.

Neither party desiring to make further interrogatories or producing other witnesses, I accordingly close this testimony, and certify that the foregoing is a true statement of answers given by the witnesses as they were respectively produced and examined before me this day.

Given under my hand and seal this 5th day of January, in the year of our Lord eighteen hundred and sixty-seven.

PETER BAKER,
Justice of the Peace, of the State of
Maryland, in and for Allegany county.

STATE OF MARYLAND,
Allegany County, to wit.

I hereby certify, that Peter Baker, Esq., before whom the annexed acknowledgments was made, and whose genuine signature thereto appears, was, at the date thereof, a Justice of the Peace in and for the State and County aforesaid, duly commissioned and sworn, and authorized by law to administer oaths and take acknowledgments.

[SEAL] In testimony whereof, I hereunto subscribe my name, and affix the seal of the Circuit Court for Allegany county, this 5th day of January, 1867.

HORACE RESLEY,
Clerk of the Circuit Court for
Allegany county.

[U. S. 5 ct. Stamp.

www.ingramcontent.com/pod-product-compliance
Lightning Source LLC
Chambersburg PA
CBHW020800020726
47495CB00008B/2517